THE SIGNAL
Mike Duke

Artwork by Mike Duke utilizing Midjourney AI and digital editing software

Edited by Lisa Lee Tone

ACKNOWLEDGMENTS

Massive props to my kickass editor, Lisa Lee Tone, and everyone who beta read this book for me and gave feedback. I'd also like to extend a special thank you to Chris Miller for beta reading The Signal and offering a blurb packed full of extraordinary praise that absolutely blew me away!

Lastly, I'd like to give a huge shout out to my loyal supporters on Patreon and all my fans who encourage me regularly to keep this writing dream alive. You all mean so very much to me.

PRAISE FOR THE SIGNAL

"That was a phenomenal ending! Something really special and awe-inspiring. On the level with the ending of 2001: A Space Odyssey. Definitely one of the best finales I've read in many years, and I think it MAKES the book."

-- *Chris Miller, author of The Damned Place, Dust, and the upcoming cyberpunk dystopian thriller The SONS of THUNDER*

CONTENTS

ESTHER NAVARRO SAT at her workstation aboard the mining scout vessel The Evangeline, monitoring the data that streamed across the three computer screens arrayed before her. Daddy Long Legs' sensors were constantly gathering an immense amount of information and relaying it to their ship. Density and Hardness readouts. A variety of metallurgy reports. Ambient energy, if any. Gravitational fluctuations and anomalies. Radiation emissions.

She picked up her coffee cup, leaned back in the chair, and

sipped the hot liquid. Her eyes wandered to the top right corner of the far-right screen. There, she focused in on a small bar graph, which would indicate if Daddy Long Legs detected organic material of any kind. In the five years she'd been working this job, Esther had never once seen it rise above zero.

Not once.

We're all alone out here, she thought, and consciously noted she thought that every time she happened to pay that particular readout any mind.

Another screen was split between the Daddy Long Legs POV camera feed and a Doppler SONAR map of everything within a hundred meters of the drone. Esther's attention waned. Her eyes glazed over and stared in between her computer screens at a tattoo of a snarling wolf, its murderous eyes staring back at her from the upper arm of her coworker Ariana, whose workstation was opposite her own.

Esther jostled her head, attempting to rattle the contents out of their drowsy state, then downed several gulps of coffee. After setting the cup down, she screwed both eyes with her knuckles. Sufficiently stirred from her intermittent slumber, she shifted her attention to the live video feed and watched as meters of brown rock slid rapidly by before the camera focused on another nearby asteroid. When it leapt into space, Esther's stomach lurched mildly. After all this time, the first-person perception of the Daddy Long Legs jumping into the void of space still got her sometimes, usually when she was tired or sleepy, but once it landed on its chosen target, she felt better.

Esther toggled between the POV cam on Daddy Long Legs and the camera on the carrier drone following it around. The screen showed the disc shaped body of Daddy Long Legs with its spindly limbs skittering across the asteroid surface as it took readings. When it was ready to move to another, its legs flexed, compressed, then extended in a brief explosive contraction calculated to deliver the drone to its next target.

Ariana piloted the carrier drone shadowing Daddy Long Legs

while monitoring his operating system and mechanical stats, ensuring he performed optimally for the duration of this scouting expedition.

Esther yawned. A few seconds later, Ariana did as well, but Esther did not notice. Ariana kicked Esther's foot beneath their workstations, raised her hands above the screens between them, and signed, "Knock that shit off," to Esther.

Esther laughed, then spoke as she signed the words, her voice possessing the discordant tone of someone born deaf.

"It's time for our lunch break, Ariana," Esther said. "Finish this one up, then bring Daddy Long Legs back on board. We'll launch for round two after we eat and take our four-hour sleep cycle. I need some rest."

Ariana raised her hand again and signed, "Okay."

It was the vibrations that woke Esther, not the sound of the signal itself like the others. A deep bass rumbled in her torso, much like a cat lying on her chest purring, except mixed in were light tapping sensations as well—sometimes single taps, one after another at steady intervals, other times a string of them overlapping at varying rhythms and tempos, as if a jazz drummer had suddenly been cut loose.

Esther's eyelids slowly lifted when she first felt the vibrations. She looked around, but there was nothing in her room to explain it. She laid back and closed her eyes, controlling her breathing so she could focus on where the feeling was coming from.

It was everywhere, it seemed. She couldn't determine any one specific direction to track its origin. She touched the metal frame of her bunk bed with one hand to sit up, and froze. The vibrations and clicks strengthened. She reached with her other hand and touched the wall. The strength of the sensations escalated a slight bit more.

Esther rolled over to look under her and see if Ariana was awake in the bottom bunk. Her roommate was sitting up and glancing around. Esther touched her shoulder, and Ariana jumped.

"Do you feel that?" Esther signed and said simultaneously.

"Feel it?" Ariana asked. "A little. But I can hear it clearly."

"What's it sound like?" Esther asked.

Ariana and Esther had developed a close relationship working together despite coming from two ends of a cultural schism. Ariana had lost her hearing as a child due to an illness and later had it cybernetically repaired so she could hear again. Esther, on the other hand, was raised by her mother to embrace Deaf Culture. "You are not broken," her mother would always say. "Deafness is simply a different way of experiencing the human journey. You don't need to be fixed."

Esther struggled to accept her mother's views in high school. She longed to hear music and share the experience with her friends in the same way they did, to know the songs and be able to discuss them on the same level of detail with her hearing companions. It was her obsession for a time, and drove a wedge between her and her mother for a time. But later, when she went to a college for the deaf, she finally immersed herself in Deaf Culture and embraced the community and camaraderie, as well as the new sense of identity she gained from it. She knew some within her community looked down on those who viewed their deafness as a disability to be fixed and didn't accept them the same way. But Esther understood the draw and was more willing to live and let live—she still found herself longing to hear music at times. So, Esther and Ariana had bonded easily over their shared background, and Ariana was still fluent in sign language.

Despite Esther's ability to read lips fairly well, Ariana enjoyed the practice, so they signed to each other as much as possible. Most of the crew went out of their way to learn at least the essentials of sign language once Esther joined them.

"Low volume," Ariana said and signed. "Deep bass. Modulating frequency. And some kind of clicking sounds mixed in."

"Can you tell where it's coming from?" Esther was curious and annoyed at the same time. Each click felt like someone plucking a guitar string in her head.

"No," Ariana admitted. "But we better figure it out. Could be something wrong with the ship, but even if the ship's fine, that shit is gonna drive me nuts if we can't make it stop."

Esther touched the side of her index finger to her head, then touched the sides of her index fingers together. "Agreed." She climbed down to the floor and slipped her shoes on.

Together, Esther and Ariana walked out into the hall to begin searching the surrounding area of the ship for the source of the sound. Two of their crewmates already stood in the corridor looking around, confusion and frustration on their faces as well.

"What the hell is that noise?" Bryan asked, tugging up his pants with one hand to cover his butt crack and spare everyone the uncomfortable sight. "Sounds like two whales fucking while a bunch of cicadas serenade their fat asses." He ran his hands through thick bushy hair and yawned. "I was trying to get a little beauty sleep while manning the helm during y'all's sleep cycle, but goddamn, that sound is enough to wake the dead."

"That's a shame, hombre," Carlos said to his heavyset crewmate, "'cause you sure do need that extra beauty. Dayum!" He backhand slapped Bryan on the upper arm and laughed.

Bryan cut him a look and cocked one eyebrow. "Laugh it up, see if I give you any more of my stash."

"Woah, woah, woah, now," Carlos said, and quickly raised his hands up in front of him, palms forward. "No reason to get dramatic, mi amigo." He smiled, then pointed both index fingers at Bryan with a wink. "I don't care what you look like. Nothing but love, peace, and chicken grease for you, my man." He closed one fist, thumped it against his muscular chest twice, and extended it toward Bryan, who grinned, thumped a fist against his own chest twice, and then bumped fists with Carlos.

"For fuck's sake, guys," Ariana said, hands on her hips, staring at Bryan and Carlos. "Can we knock off the machismo and figure out where the hell that sound is coming from and what's causing it? You know, before we end up floating in space or something equally deadly."

Carlos's hands flew back up. "No problem, muchacha."

Bryan just shrugged and grunted, then cocked his head and listened. After a minute, he shook his head slowly. "I can't pinpoint it. Ariana, you got a decibel meter device in that extensive kit of yours, right?"

"Sorry, no," she replied.

Bryan grunted again and looked around. "Damn."

"Hey," Esther said, and everyone looked at her. "Let me try," she said and signed. "I can feel the clicking. Maybe it will get stronger the closer I get to the source."

"Sounds like as good a plan as any," Bryan said, nodding.

Miko walked through the doorway leading to the rear of the ship and the engine room right then, and yawned. "Y'all hear this weird noise?" she asked. Her straight black hair was pulled back in a ponytail that hung halfway down to her waist. Big brown doe eyes with a distinctive Asian American shape stared at her shipmates while she tried to rouse herself from the deep sleep still firmly holding on to her by the shirt tail.

"Yeah, Miko," Bryan said. "We all hear it."

He caught himself and looked briefly at Esther, then added. "Well … she *feels* it. We all *hear* it."

"Well," Miko said, "it's definitely stronger back that way. Shit woke me up from my sleep cycle. What the hell is it?"

"No clue yet," Carlos said.

"Okay." Esther spoke up, ready to find the noise and make the clicking stop. "If it's stronger at the rear of the ship, let's go check that way." She walked past them and through the doorway, heading for the rear of the ship. She would spearhead this operation herself if no one else was going to make something happen.

It didn't take long for Esther to track down the epicenter of the vibrations and clicks. She placed a hand against the corridor wall as she walked. The vibrations from the bass and the light impacts of the clicking sounds increased in strength until she passed a short distance beyond the midship point. As she moved further toward the rear of the ship, they began to dwindle in intensity. Esther did an about-face and returned to where the clicking and bass felt the strongest. She turned in a circle, trying to pinpoint it.

"It's strongest right here," Esther declared. "What do you think, Mr. Engineer?" she asked Bryan.

"Fuck if I know. This makes no sense," Bryan stated. "There's nothing of any significant mechanical function in this area. Just pipes transporting water and oxygen throughout the ship. Definitely nothing to do with the ship's engines. That's for sure."

Esther shrugged. "I don't know," she signed. "But it's strongest here."

Ariana glanced about, her face scrunched up in perplexity, until she looked upward, and suddenly, her face opened like a flower with excitement. She turned to face Esther so the girl could read her lips.

"Esther!" she said, placing a hand on the wall beside her. "You can feel it vibrating in the ship's walls, right?"

Esther nodded.

"Guys!" Ariana clapped her hands and pointed upward with both index fingers, her excitement palpable. "What's right above us?"

Each of her crewmates gave a vacant stare, mental gears turning but getting nowhere.

"The comms array antennae!" she declared loudly. "The antennae must be picking up some kind of signal, and it's being relayed or grounded somehow into the ship."

"What?" Carlos said, face screwed up in disbelief. "A signal would have to be strong as fuck to do something like. So powerful that it overwhelms the receiver system and the safety mechanisms divert the signal so it overflows into the ship's structure itself and doesn't blow out our comms completely. But *nothing* any of our ships use out here would have that kind of signal strength. It's impossible."

Both Ariana's eyebrows shot up, and her lips pursed and curled in on themselves. She looked as if she could explode with excitement. "Exactly!" she exclaimed.

"Holy fuck," Bryan said. "Are you serious?" He paused for a moment, staring at Ariana, then swallowed and finished the thought. "You think that's some kind of extraterrestrial signal, don't you?"

Ariana's head bobbled up and down rapidly. "I do," she confessed.

"Hold on," Esther signed. "You mean to tell me you believe there's something alien out there making contact? Really?"

Ariana nodded.

"How?" Esther asked. "How can you believe that? You know as well as I that in all the years humankind has been travelling out here, not once has there been an alien life form detected or anything remotely resembling alien communication confirmed."

"Well," Ariana responded, "I'm not a close-minded person. I'm willing to accept there may be other life out there. In fact, I don't just believe it's possible, I believe it's quite probable that alien life exists. Just because there hasn't been anything discovered yet doesn't mean they're not out there. The universe is *beyond huge*. To rule it out and call it impossible is not scientific at all."

Esther shook her head. "Fine. Just make sure you do look at it with an *objective eye* and don't try to squeeze a square peg in a round hole. If it fits, it fits; if it doesn't, it doesn't."

Ariana's brow furrowed and chin tucked. "Of course," she said, her contempt for the implied insult displayed on her face as clearly as it was detectable by the others in her tone of voice. "But first things first. We need to get to the bridge, pull up the comms program, then record the signal. After that, we can analyze it."

"Y'all do that," Miko said. "I'm gonna throw in some ear plugs or something and try to get back to sleep. That bed is calling to me still."

Without another word, Miko walked off, and Ariana turned and headed for the bridge, Esther close behind. Bryan and Carlos glanced at one another.

"I better tell the captain," Bryan said. "She'll want to know."

"You do that, bro," Carlos said. "Better you than me. She likes you, for some reason."

Carlos bumped Bryan's upper arm with his forearm and walked off.

Bryan stood at the door to Captain Roza Morozov's quarters and pushed the call button. *If ever a name fit,* Bryan thought, *hers does.* Roses have thorns, and the name Morozov, he had learned during the two years he worked with her, meant bitter cold.

But even that was an understatement. The woman was a jagged icicle. No doubt about it.

She was at home out here, away from the vast majority of society; and even amongst their small crew, most of them didn't dare speak to her, afraid she'd bite their heads off, metaphorically if not literally. Except for Esther. She would sign with Esther, neither of them speaking, just silently communicating. And she'd talk to Bryan. For whatever reason, she seemed to tolerate him better than the others, crass humor and all.

When she didn't respond, Bryan flipped up a small panel beside the door and punched in an override code, which only he had been given by the captain. It shut off the music being transmitted to her cochlear implants, which helped shut out the ship noises and allowed her to sleep better. He counted to five, then hit the call button again. This time, a voice answered.

"What the fuck do you want, Bryan?" she said in a heavy Russian accent. "And what's that goddamn noise?"

"Hate to disturb you, boss, but that noise is why I woke you. Ariana says it's some kind of signal, and apparently, it's strong as hell. The ship's humming like a goddamn tuning fork. Oh, and the best part ... Ariana thinks the signal is *not* terrestrial in origin."

He worded that carefully. He did not want to use the word extraterrestrial with the captain after waking her up.

"Vut?!?" she asked, confused. "She thinks we have an alien talking to us, huh?"

The door opened. Captain Morozov stood before Bryan, her breath rank with the vodka fermenting in her mouth over the last six hours. Her hair was short, spiky, and unkempt. Bryan took a step back and looked down, trying to distance his nose from the odor, only to notice her nipples pressing through the thin brown under-shirt she wore.

"Something got your attention there, Bryan?" Morozov asked him, a bit perturbed.

He looked up, looked her in the eyes, and shook his head. "Not anymore, boss. Sorry, it's just the nature of the organism, ya know? Pokey nipples are like fishhooks to a man's eyeballs. You got me there for a second. I'm good now, though." He gave a mock salute and flashed a crooked grin.

"Unh huh," she grunted. Morozov turned and grabbed a sturdy double-breasted jacket and slipped it on. "Better?" she asked sarcastically.

"Yes, ma'am," Bryan said and turned away. "Without the jacket, they're a health hazard, for sure. You could've put my eye out with those things."

Morozov smacked Bryan in the back of the head, the impact firm but not overly hard.

"Oh!" Bryan exclaimed then rubbed his head. "Yeah. I deserved that."

"Yes, you did," said Morozov, squeezing past him, a grin momentarily stretching her face before disappearing. "Now, let's go see what Ariana's figured out before that sound drives me batshit crazy."

Bryan nodded and fell in behind Morozov. *Damn*, he thought, watching her walk, *that woman has one magnificent turd cutter. Too bad she's colder than a witch's tit in a brass bra on a winter day. Freeze my pecker right off on first contact. No doubt about it.*

CAPTAIN MOROZOV WALKED ONTO THE BRIDGE WITH BRYAN BEHIND her. Everyone stood in a semi-circle behind Ariana, leaning over her and her console.

"What do we have there, Ariana?" Morozov asked, walking up to stand behind the woman. Carlos moved over and backed out of the way, relinquishing his space without a word. Esther stood to her right. Morozov looked down at the shorter woman and signed, "Hi, Esther."

Esther smiled and signed back, "Hi, Captain."

Carlos watched the exchange and shook his head.

"Captain," Ariana said. "Esther was able to determine where the noise was coming from, and I suspected it was a signal coming through our antennae array and not something on board the ship causing the noises. I've accessed comms and confirmed it. It is definitely a transmission of some sort, and the signal strength is through the friggin roof. That's why it's both audible and physically palpable. I'm going to turn down our antenna's reception strength now, see if it helps."

Ariana pulled up a soundboard on her screen and made several adjustments. When she was done, the noise was much lower in volume and the clicking sounds were no longer audible.

Esther breathed a sigh of relief. She could hardly feel them now.

"Damn, Ariana," Bryan said. "That's hella better. Now it's just the sound of two whales fucking sans the cicada serenade."

Morozov cut her eyes at Bryan. "Your brain …" she began and paused a moment before holding up a palm and circling it in the air in front of him, "and everything about you … I'll never understand it, Bryan."

"You know that old saying, right, boss?" Bryan asked, a glint of humor in his eyes. "'Genius is never understood in its own time.'"

Bryan chuckled while Morozov guffawed once, then said, "I don't think that's the problem we have here, Bryan." Morozov was grinning, though, when she turned back to the console and looked down at Ariana.

"Can you tell where it's coming from?" Morozov asked.

"Not yet," Ariana admitted, "but I'm going to assign a bot program to figure it out. Hopefully in the next couple of hours, the bot can track the signal to the source and triangulate a location."

"Good," Morozov said. "I know you're excited about aliens and first contact, but I'm more about finding salvage or something that could make for a big payday. But maybe, if we're lucky, we'll both find something we value." She patted Ariana's shoulder. "Keep me posted," Morozov said to her, then looked at Bryan and nodded. Before turning away from the group, though, Morozov touched Esther's arm and signed, "Goodbye." Esther returned the gesture.

"Okay, back to work or back to sleep," Morozov said, then headed to her room to finish her own sleep cycle.

"Ariana," Bryan said, "If you're gonna be up playing with this for a while, I'm gonna turn in and get some sleep."

"You go, boy," she said. "I'll be here."

ESTHER FELT TIRED BUT COULDN'T FALL ASLEEP, SO SHE RETURNED TO the bridge and joined Ariana to keep her company. She kicked back in her chair and propped her feet up, angling herself where she could see Ariana's face through an opening between their monitors. Her coworker was wide awake, eyes fixed on the screen, actively scanning multiple sources of information.

It was obvious to Esther that Ariana was actively chasing the signal to its source with the help of the bot program. Her coworker was a relentless hunter, determined to zero in on her quarry and pin it down. An admirable quality, for sure, though she could be a bit zealous in some of her beliefs at times, in Esther's opinion.

But can't we all, she thought, one side of her mouth twitching upward.

Excitement painted Ariana's face. She was almost salivating. Esther knew the woman wouldn't rest until she ran it to ground like a pack of hounds pursuing the scent of their prey.

As Esther watched Ariana, she slowly drifted off to sleep.

2

"Woooh!" Ariana cried out and slapped the desktop at her workspace.

Esther didn't stir, so the woman balled her fists and banged on her desktop again, then did a rapid-fire drumroll with her hands, both of which caused her and Esther's shared desk to vibrate wildly.

In Esther's mind, in that moment, she suddenly dreamed the ship was shaking itself apart and woke with a start, eyes wide, head twisting back and forth as she dropped her feet to the floor. She spotted Ariana standing up and peeking over the monitors, a huge smile spread across her face.

"Oh, for fuck's sake," Esther said and signed to Ariana. "You scared the shit out of me."

"Sorry," Ariana signed, "but I had to wake you up."

"Did you locate the source of the signal?" Esther signed, then rubbed her eyes.

"Yes," Ariana exclaimed aloud, holding up one fist and rapidly giving what looked like three raps on a door hanging in the air to sign *yes* as well. "Come and see!"

Esther lurched to her feet and hurried around to stand beside Ariana where she could see the woman's terminal.

"Here," Ariana signed, looking at Esther, then pointed to the screen and tapped a spot she had marked.

Esther leaned in and looked closer. "Is it nearby anything else?" she asked.

"No," Ariana signed. "That's the weirdest part. It's a few light years inside of this small cosmic void we're working near. It's literally empty ... just space dust and dark energy. There's *nothing* of significance nearby."

"Could it be another ship, then?" Esther signed "A distress beacon, maybe?"

"It could possibly be a ship," Ariana signed and said, looking at Esther, "but it's *definitely* not a distress beacon."

"How are you so sure?" Esther signed, her face scrunched up in confusion.

"This is where things get a little weird," Ariana confessed. "I've been studying the signal, analyzing its structure and makeup. Bryan wasn't too far off in describing it as the sound of two whales fucking."

Ariana laughed at the face Esther made, then continued. "Except it might better have been described as an orgy of whales."

She laughed again at her own joke as Esther's nose wrinkled in disgust and she made an "Ewwww" sound.

"What do you mean?" Esther asked, looking as if she might not even want to know.

"Well, the signal is made up of several different sounds broadcast together." Ariana's voice rose in pitch and volume as she spoke, while her face and hands became more animated in expressions and movement. "There seems to be one always in the background, and then the others rotate through, causing the signal sound to change fairly often. It's what's referred to as a binaural beat. Each sound registers at a distinct hertz."

Ariana's excitement was contagious, but Esther was at a loss as to what the significance might be.

"I'm sorry," Esther signed, "but I have no idea what any of this means. Can you explain *why* this is important?"

"Okay," Ariana said and turned in her seat to fully face Esther. "Different sounds affect our bodies and minds differently. The first one I isolated is the one sound that's constant. It registers at 417 hertz. This is the same frequency used in certain types of mantra chanting. It's also considered by many to be the primordial sound of the universe."

Esther's left eyebrow rose, and her head recoiled slightly. Ariana picked up on Esther's reflexive rejection of the concept but ignored it and continued.

"People who believe in the power of sound say this frequency reverberates in every cell making up the human form. It's capable of optimizing cellular function and cleansing both body and mind of negativity and blocks. It can also enable change and has even been shown to help people overcome past trauma."

"Wow," Esther signed, trying to hide her skepticism so as not to offend Ariana. "That's pretty crazy. How do you know this stuff?"

"Well, I took a semester in college on Eastern and Indian religions and studied their meditation techniques in detail with an emphasis on recording biofeedback. We spent a month on this topic alone and were guinea pigs during several practice sessions. Our instructor brought in a few different consultants to give us a genuine experience, but they also tested their hypothesis on how different frequencies would affect us. They exposed us to one frequency at a time during meditation exercises and while we slept, then they had us answer a series of questions both immediately after each meditative session and every morning after sleeping with the sound all night. They even taught us a few chants and gave us extra credit for any additional time spent meditating and chanting followed by giving them feedback on each session."

"That sounds pretty cool," Esther said, her disbelief waning before Ariana's first-hand experience. A twinge of envy creeped into her heart. The more time she spent out here in the void of space, the more often she found herself wishing she could experi-

CHAPTER 2 | 17

ence music in its fullness. The silence could be oppressive and isolating. At times, it made her feel disconnected from the universe, a castaway in the black abyss.

"It was," Ariana acknowledged, then, seeing the look on Esther's face, added, "I could teach you one or two of the chants sometime. Some of them are very low and vibrate in your throat. You can feel it just as much as you hear it. You might like the sensation and find it relaxing. I know I do."

"I'd like that," Esther replied. "What other frequencies did you isolate?"

"All right," Ariana continued. "Here's the other frequencies I've found so far that are oscillating within the signal and what they are supposed to be good for."

She tapped on the pad and pulled up the list she had created, looking at it periodically for reference as she signed the information to Esther.

"I had to look most of these up in the ship's database," she told Esther. "I forgot most of this stuff several years ago. It's a lot of info, but it will all make sense when I'm done, so bear with me." Ariana gave an apologetic half smile, one side of her mouth curving up.

"Anyway, here's the list. First, 174 hertz helps relieve physical pain and makes us feel more safe and secure. Second, 285 hertz helps the body heal and grants a sense of wellbeing and optimism. Third, 396 hertz helps free people from fear and guilt, lowers defense mechanisms, aids in focusing on goals and achieving them. Fourth, 528 hertz helps with emotional and physical healing, harmonizes body and mind, and empowers us to release inner conflicts and forgive others, which decreases depression and fear and increases inner peace. Some say it can even repair our DNA."

Ariana paused then signed, "You good so far? Still with me?"

"Yes," Esther signed emphatically. "My attention span is longer than that. Get on with it."

Ariana laughed and continued.

"Okay, fifth, 639 hertz improves intercellular connectivity and communication with the environment. It's believed it can improve relationships as well. Sixth, 741 hertz enhances creativity and personal expression. Seventh, 852 hertz is a higher vibrational level and is often associated with pure love and light. It's supposed to open people up to spiritual experiences and enable people to return to the source of all spiritual order. And eighth, the last one I found is 963 hertz. They call this the frequency of the gods. It's supposed to create higher states of consciousness by activating the pineal gland, or what some refer to as opening the third eye. They think it provides mystical perception and connects us to a divine intuition."

Ariana paused for a few seconds and shifted in her seat. She shivered briefly and wrapped her arms around herself.

Esther squinted in concern, then signed, "What's wrong?"

Ariana pursed her lips. They twitched, shifting to one side of her mouth and then the other as she considered Esther's words.

"It's just ... there's something I realized that's freaking me out a little ..."

"What is it?" Esther signed.

"The signal composition is rather odd," Ariana signed. "It's composed of *all nine* of the Solfeggio frequencies. I mean, you can generally find these in tracks produced for meditation, relaxation, to aid in falling asleep, and stuff like that, but what the hell are they doing out here in the middle of goddamn space, light years away from Earth or any other planet or star? Plus, the signal strength is *off the fucking charts*. I mean, it's stronger than *any* signal broadcast I've *ever* encountered ... It's just all so ... *fucking weird. So goddamn weird.*"

Esther could clearly see concern etched deep into Ariana's brow and around her eyes. They sat in silence together for a short time, then Esther asked another question.

"How far away is it from us?"

"Not too far, actually. We're currently working about one light year away from the edge of this void here." Ariana tapped the screen, then dragged her finger to where she had marked the signal. "With the FTL engines at three-quarter power, we could be there in no more than five days, easy."

"Wow," Esther signed. "That's not far at all."

"Tempting, huh?" Ariana asked, her eyes alive with a light Esther hadn't seen before. It quickly dispelled the fear and concern on her face from moments before. There was an obvious tug of war at work within her friend.

"Yeah," Esther said, "tempting." But something inside her was uneasy at the idea. She shivered, and her stomach fluttered, like butterflies rising up through her throat. Esther stared at the screen for several seconds, and then suddenly, the signal changed. She felt the deep base frequencies begin vibrating within her whole body even as the computer screen reflected the additions to the original signal.

"Holy shit!" Ariana spat and sat up, leaning forward in her chair to stare at the readout on her computer. She clicked and swiped and analyzed for a few minutes as Esther stood behind her, watching. After verifying the results, she turned to Esther.

"Can you feel the new elements added to the signal?" Ariana asked her out loud while signing.

Esther nodded.

"They're all super low frequencies. Alpha, Delta, and Theta wave modulations rumbling in the background beneath everything now." Ariana's eyebrows shot up and her voice raised in pitch. "I need to look up what effect they're supposed to have on people! Hold on."

Ariana's fingers typed at a furious pace, and her right fingertip would periodically reach over and zip back and forth along the mousepad, then tap it with impatient force before she returned to the keyboard. As she located each piece of information, she signed it to Esther in a hurry then focused on the computer screen until she found the next thing she was searching for and paused to sign again.

"Accelerates learning of new information through memorization ... Allows one to absorb information passively ... Increases creativity, enhances serotonin release, elevates mood, increases arousal, acts as a stimulant ... Provides relief from lack of sleep ... Reduces headaches ... Improves subconscious correlation ... Increases clarity, focus, and awareness ... Relaxes the mind, increases focus, centers the spirit, and provides improved mental stability."

Ariana studied the screen, correlating information and connecting the dots. After several minutes of silence, her face went slack in apparent disbelief.

"This is nuts, Esther," she signed and said. "It seems as if this signal was designed with the express purpose of helping a person access some kind of Zen-like state of learning along with a paradise-level state of bliss, all while enabling your cells to heal themselves and expanding the mind and body's capabilities, free from the damaging effects life subjects us to constantly."

Ariana stared back at the screen for several seconds, then looked up at Esther. "It sounds ... heavenly," she confessed, "if you think about it."

Esther could see the beginning of blissful feelings poking out on Ariana's face already. It looked worthy of envy on one hand, but something felt unnatural about it on the other. Either way, Esther's radar was up. She glanced back down at her friend's face.

Ariana had closed her eyes and was sitting silent and perfectly still. Her eyeballs rolled all about behind her lids. Esther touched the girl's shoulder, and Ariana jumped a little and looked at Esther, eyes wide open.

"Esther, this is freaking me out," Ariana confided. "Earlier, I thought I was starting to feel a little more energetic, more centered, and full of positive vibes, ya know? But now, I can't remember the last time I felt *this damn good* ... I mean, this peaceful, this focused. I feel amazing. Can you feel any difference too?"

Esther shook her head side to side and signed, "No." Her face looked dejected at this additional form of isolation, but her mind was torn between jealousy and a gnawing dread in her gut that assured her she was better off without it.

Later, Esther would look back and realize *this* was the moment when the path to hell made itself known, an angel of light with a dark hunger leading them onward into an inescapable abyss.

3

CAPTAIN MOROZOV WOKE from her sleep cycle feeling more refreshed, invigorated, and free of her normal body aches and pains than she had in years. She set about brushing her teeth and fixing her hair with no feelings of frustration or depression, and soon found herself humming a playful tune. She was riding high and hadn't experienced genuine feelings of hope like this since she was a child.

Despite being in the darkest depths of space, Morozov felt bathed in light and love and the promise of community. So much so that instead of remaining in her quarters until someone, usually Bryan, came to get her, she decided to head for the crew breakroom and grab coffee and heat up a pre-packaged breakfast meal. As she made her way there, she found herself hoping the crew would be doing the same. She actually *felt* the desire for company.

Morozov was delighted to find most of her crewmates there already, squeezing around one another as they hustled and bustled about, preparing food and drink. Conversation flowed effortlessly from every mouth present. As she entered the room, no heads turned in shock, no mouths ceased to speak. Her presence was both welcome and not considered novel or odd by anyone present despite her track record in the past. Bryan poured her coffee. Ariana and Miko offered her food, and Carlos gave up his seat so she could sit at the head of the table.

She wondered why on Earth she had ever sequestered herself in her quarters when so many kind people were happy to see her. Morozov looked around. Only one thing darkened the moment.

"Where's Esther?" Morozov asked.

"Still sleeping like a little baby roo in its momma's pouch," Bryan said.

"Can you go check on her, Bryan?" Morozov asked. "See if she's up to joining us. We need to discuss our current situation." The captain smiled.

"You bet, boss! I'm on it." Bryan gave her a mock salute, stood, hitched up his britches so the crack of his ass didn't scar everyone present, and left to check on Esther.

Morozov sipped at her coffee, drinking it for the taste rather than the caffeine. In between speaking with Ariana, she nibbled at the protein rations the girls shared with her, though she wasn't particularly hungry. She noticed they, too, ate very little.

"I don't know about you guys," Morozov said, "but I feel like I could take on the world right now. Run a marathon, dance all night, hike Everest, fly across the galaxy, read Plato's works in one sitting, or solve quadratic equations from morning to night. Anything."

"You too?" Ariana said. "I thought it was just me at first, but then I noticed everyone appears to be feeling far better than normal. You know, more energized and invigorated, and more intellectually stimulated too, it seems. Am I right?" Ariana looked at Miko and Carlos.

Both of them nodded vigorously.

"Absolutely," Carlos said. "I swear I've never experienced such a physical and mental rush. My focus is laser sharp, and my body seems primed for action. I could fight, fuck, or run for hours the way I feel right now." Carlos winked at Miko. She didn't blush, nor did she look offended.

Ariana smacked Carlos on the arm.

"What the hell, man?" she said, her mama bear persona coming out quickly. "You know Miko's the quiet, introvert type. What the hell's wrong with you? You've never done that shit before."

"Um ... I don't know," he said. "I guess I just feel ... I don't know ... I guess more at ease, accepted, able to relax my guard and say what I was thinking and feeling. Honestly, I felt the same vibe from her." He turned to look at Miko, who now was blushing a bit.

"Miko?" Ariana said. "If you feel different, I'll back down."

Miko took a deep breath and blew it out slowly through her nose, her face smiling and at peace. "I do feel different," she said. "I feel *alive*, like I've never felt before. I have ... an acute desire to connect physically *and* emotionally with another person. With Carlos in particular right now." Her features softened, and a teasing seductiveness peeked out from behind a vivacious countenance. "Every inch of my body feels like rocket fuel is coursing through it." She looked directly at Carlos. "I don't care about fighting or running, but I'd *love* to fuck for hours. I'm horny as hell right now. Swear to God."

Miko giggled at her blunt confession and covered her mouth for a second, then grabbed Carlos's hand and squeezed it. She winked at him and sucked at one side of her bottom lip without thinking. He nodded his head in complete approval, eyes wide and filling with excitement.

"All right, chica," he said, raising one eyebrow and trying to be cool. "We *are* on the same page."

Morozov laughed. Ariana's eyebrows were stuck in her hairline.

"All right, you two," Morozov said. "Get a room unless you want an audience that cheers and will critique you based on technique and exuberance. But first, we all need to talk."

Bryan and Esther entered the breakroom.

"Found her, boss," he said, jerking a thumb in Esther's direction behind him. "She was snuggled down like a bug in a rug underneath that blanket." He turned around and signed to Esther, "Sit down, I'll bring you some coffee."

"Thanks," Esther signed and slid in next to Morozov, who

signed, "Hello," to her. Esther waved and smiled then rubbed her eyes.

"How do you feel right now, Esther?" Morozov signed.

Esther pressed her lips together and tilted her head from side to side.

"Weird," Esther replied. "One minute I feel energized, and the next I want to hibernate. One minute I feel like sharing my life with y'all, and the next I want to be a hermit and stay in my room. One minute, highly motivated to do stuff; the next, fighting apathy. I feel like a yo-yo." She paused, then, balling both fists up, brought them to her chest and let them fall, hands opening, while simultaneously blowing air out through her mouth to sign, "It's exhausting."

Morozov looked genuinely sad for Esther. "Why do you think that is?" she asked.

Esther shrugged, then raised both hands, palms up.

"I think I may know," Ariana said. "Or at least have an idea. Since Esther can't hear but her body does detect the vibrations, she's not receiving the full effect that we are. I think it's the equivalent of someone turning the power off and on, but each time it's on and she feels great, the next time the power is turned off it's a bigger crash. Cycle this multiple times per hour, and you've got a recipe for feeling like utter shit."

"Oh my God," Esther signed. "That makes perfect sense."

"Is there anything we can do for her?" Morozov asked, looking from Ariana to Miko.

"I don't think so," said Ariana. "There's no way to isolate Esther from the signal. Even a soundproof room wouldn't matter on this ship because some amount of the vibrations would still reach her. It might help some, but there's no guarantee. So, other than putting her in a suit and keeping her tethered outside in space for a couple of hours at a shot, I can't think of anything."

Esther's mouth gaped. Ariana laughed at her and so did Morozov.

"We wouldn't do that to you unless you truly wanted it," Morozov assured Esther.

Morozov turned to focus her gaze on Miko, their ship doc, and waited.

"Well," Miko began, "I can try giving her some stimulants, as well as a couple of mood-stabilizing drugs. It might help balance things out a little."

"Okay, Miko," said Morozov. "When we're done here, make it happen."

"Will do, Captain."

"Now," Morozov signed and said aloud, looking around at her crew, "we need to talk about our current situation with this signal. What it might be. How it's affecting us. And what are we going to do?" Morozov looked at Ariana. "Ariana, can you explain to everyone your professional assessment of this signal as the science and communications officer on board?"

Ariana nodded, then proceeded to recap for everyone the nature of the signal and its probable effects on everyone based on both her studies, just as she did for Esther. Afterwards, they compared each crewmember's account of how they personally felt they had changed since the ship started receiving the signal. Everyone agreed they were being significantly impacted by the signal. With the exception of Esther and her experience of on and off effects, the signal was overwhelmingly positive, a veritable godsend in how it made the rest of them feel physically, emotionally, and mentally.

"I haven't felt this good in my whole damn life," Carlos proclaimed. "My whole body feels vibrant and saturated with …" he paused, searching for sufficient words. "I know it sounds corny, but the best description I can think of is life and light. I feel charged, hyper-charged even, like something is pumping life energy into me and every cell in my body is a better conductor and repository of that energy than any other human being has ever been before in all our history as a species … If that makes any sense to y'all?"

Everyone but Esther nodded in complete agreement. She had managed to read Carlos's lips and understood what he said but had no reference point to really comprehend what he meant. She wished she did. She felt like utter shit. Sleep seemed to be the only potential escape from this roller coaster of physical fatigue, emotional angst and dread, and the equivalent of ADHD on steroids mixed with moments of crystal-clear clarity before it crumbled and a brain fog of colossal density enveloped her in its grip.

Esther covered her eyes and rubbed them vigorously. When she opened them again and looked up at Morozov next to her, she couldn't believe what she saw Morozov saying.

"I think we should set a course for the source of the signal," Morozov said and signed, "and find out what it is. All in favor?"

Morozov raised her hand, and everyone else quickly lifted theirs in the air in agreement. Everyone except for Esther. Her mouth gaped.

Morozov looked at Esther directly and signed, "What say you, Esther? Do you want to go with us?"

The phrasing of the question struck Esther wrong.

It made her wonder just what Morozov meant by it. She didn't ask, "Do you vote to go or not go?" She said, "Do you want to go with us?" Which implied there were one or more scenarios in which they could go and Esther would not accompany them. Without realizing it, Esther got a thousand-yard stare and her eyes narrowed to tiny slits.

But it's not as if there's any way they could go without me ... unless ... A shiver ran through Esther's gut, struck her spine, and slithered up into her skull.

Unless they leave you behind ... in an escape pod, she thought.

Fear sounded like a claxon alarm in her head at once. She tried to reason with her brain, assure it there was no way her crewmates would abandon her if she didn't want to go. But her brain was persistent.

Words mean things, her mind insisted. *We construct sentences in specific ways to communicate specific ideas,* it argued. *The implications of her words are not by accident. Even if not intentional, there's something subconscious going on there.*

Esther struggled to restrain her frantic thoughts from being driven over a cliff's edge like some herd of animals under attack and running wildly, oblivious to the deadly drop and gaping maw waiting below. Panic and dread cut the cords of logical thinking and urged her to flee at once. Anywhere, safe or not, was better than being there a second longer, her brain insisted. But Esther fought with her fears, gnashing teeth and clawing at the immaterial until she gave it substance, her fingers seizing locks of hair to twist round her bony digits and jerk and drag and subdue until she corralled the careening thoughts teeming within her head into a pen and closed the gate.

And still the work was not done. Her brain began to sort through self-preservation options, of which there were few it could imagine.

She would agree to go with them. For now.

Esther blinked and opened her eyes.

Morozov was kneeling before her, face to face, eyes full of concern.

"What's wrong?" Esther signed.

"You blanked out there for several seconds," Morozov answered. "Closed your eyes and checked out. Are you okay?"

Esther looked around. Miko stood beside her, eyes scanning Esther's face. The rest of her crewmates' faces were furrowed with concern for her.

Not enough to abandon going after the signal, though, she thought.

"I don't feel well," Esther signed. "My thoughts are scattered. Hard to focus. I need to go lay down and sleep again."

"Okay," Morozov said and signed. "Miko will go with you and give you something to try and help. Do you think you can handle tracking down the signal with us?"

Panic slammed into her heart like a wooden stake hammered into a vampire's chest. She almost shrieked in fear. She closed her eyes again, but this time on purpose, then took a deep breath and opened them. She nodded.

"I'll be okay," she assured Morozov. "I can handle it. I just may need a lot of rest and less time at my station."

"I can work with that." Morozov touched Esther's shoulder, then stood.

"Can I ask one question, Captain?" Esther signed.

"Of course," Morozov replied.

"What about our current job? Identifying metals for retrieval within this asteroid belt? What will corporate say when they find out we've abandoned our mission?"

Morozov squatted back down and looked Esther in the eye. Her gaze was confident and exuded a hopeful positivity.

"I'm sure if we make contact with an extraterrestrial entity, they won't care a bit. They'll be ecstatic. And if we can figure out the source of this signal and how to harness and bottle this physical effect? Holy hell. They'll make us rich, 'cause everyone and their mommas will want some of what we're experiencing right now."

Morozov pointed at Esther, then at herself, and signed a circle with one hand. Holding all four fingers together she touched her thumb then flicked her index and middle fingers out, one upright, the other bent outward in the shape of a K. "We'll be okay," her hand movements communicated. She waited for Esther to nod, then smiled and stood back up again.

"All right, folks!" she called out loudly. "Set a course for the signal and full speed ahead."

Cheers rose from the others, and everyone hurried off to prepare for engaging the FTL engines, except for Miko and Esther, who headed to Miko's office before sending Esther back to bed thoroughly medicated.

4

Miko

MIKO SAT IN HER OFFICE, THE INTEGRAL DIGITAL VIDEO CAMERA INSIDE her computer pointed at the small metal pan laying on the desk before her and the scalpel resting inches away. She was ready to experiment and assess the results.

Two days ago, her curiosity had been piqued. After riding Carlos like a cowgirl hyped up on cocaine, she climbed off the bed, turned to head for the bathroom, and whacked her lower right leg against a metal toolbox Carlos left sitting out in his room away from the wall. She felt the impact, but there was no debilitating pain, no sickening nausea. When she looked down at it, she saw a large lump risen along the shin bone. The hematoma was already purple, red, and black, and the skin was broken, though not split wide open.

An hour later, it was fully healed.

Very interesting, Miko had thought. *Amazing, actually. This definitely warrants further investigation.*

She needed to conduct further testing.

So, here she was. Scalpel in right hand, left hand held over the metal pan.

"Performing incision now," she said. "Start timer."

Miko placed the scalpel blade against the pad of her left thumb, braced her right thumb on the back of her left, then pressed in and twisted her hand gripping the scalpel in a half moon path.

The blade bit through flesh as if nothing were there until it touched bone and made a scraping sound. Miko didn't flinch, didn't even wince at the self-inflicted injury. The lack of significant pain surprised her, as did her level of detachment from the injury. It was unnerving at first how she was able to injure herself for the sake of pure scientific inquiry, divorced from physical sensations or mental trepidation.

She watched the razor-thin red line open like a zipper into a puckered smile, revealing fascia, meat, globules of fatty tissue, and even a glimpse of bone.

Two seconds later, the blood flowed. It spattered into the metal pan, the sound like large drops of rain splattering in multiplicity on a tin roof.

"Incision complete. Cut to the bone. Tendon severed. I cannot bend my thumb."

Miko placed the scalpel back on her desk on a folded white cloth and sat calmly, ready to document the results. She did not sweat, nor did her skin pale at any point. She spoke aloud, describing each stage of the healing.

"One minute out," Miko noted. "Bleeding has stopped without any application of direct pressure, tourniquet, or clotting agent."

"Ten minutes out. I can see the deepest tissues knitting themselves back together.

"Twenty minutes out. The wound is slowly but steadily closing up from the inside out. The tendon has reconnected itself. I can flex my thumb again."

"Thirty minutes out. The wound is nothing more than a shallow scratch at this point."

"Thirty-three minutes out. The wound is fully closed and healed over. No indication of a scar or that there was ever an incision to begin with."

Miko turned her thumb all about, holding it up to the light on different angles as she scrutinized the skin.

"Fascinating," she said.

ARIANA

THE SIGNAL STRENGTH WAS INCREASING THE CLOSER THEY DREW NEAR the source. For two days, Ariana had tracked the numbers and watched them rise at a steady rate in ever increasing increments. By the time they reached the source, the signal strength would have tripled, at least.

She worried about Esther and how it would impact her friend and coworker, but only occasionally and never for very long.

Her brain was a laser-focused instrument now, but it was continually drawn to only a single endeavor. She yearned for knowledge. To learn so much more than she already knew. Anything else was an unwanted distraction. Even the usual no-strings-attached hook-ups she engaged in with Carlos were of no interest to her now. He had approached her once, not long after he screwed Miko. Ariana could smell the other woman's scent on him, but she felt no jealousy. She wasn't interested in Carlos. She declined. He returned the following day to pester her. Twice. She turned him down the first time to continue her studies, and the second time, she stated, emphatically, she had no desire to engage in sex with him or anyone else and suggested he try Miko or Morozov.

Carlos paled at the thought of asking Morozov to have sex with him. He shook his head in confusion.

"I don't get it," he said to Ariana. "The signal is pushing my sex drive through the roof, and my stamina is nuts! Plus, every sensation is crazy intense. I swear, sex is almost all I think about now."

"Well," Ariana said, standing to put a hand on his chest and push him out the door, "that last part doesn't sound like anything new. But, why don't you go see if it's all Miko can think about too. Now, bye-bye, and don't come ask me again. You know, don't call me, I'll call you … *if* something changes. And, of course, it's totally me, not you."

Ariana displayed a disingenuous smile as she tilted her head, then turned and went back to her desk and continued her studies. Her focused commitment had paid off. In the past two days, she had managed to speed read all of Plato and Aristotle's source material, as well as the works of Socrates, Confucius, Augustine of Hippo, Rene Descartes, David Hume, Jean Paul Sartre, Soren Kierkegaard, Niccolo Machiavelli, and Friedrich Nietzsche. She also devoured Sun Tzu's *The Art of War*, Musashi's *Book of Five Rings*, Herodotus's *Histories*, then dove into *The Iliad* and *The Odyssey* by Homer.

Ariana closed the file on the book she just finished. *Beowulf.* She'd inhaled it like a fat kid eating a piece of cake. It only took her fifteen minutes.

So intense was her focus that not only was she not feeling any sense of hunger but she was completely unaware that she hadn't felt the need for food at all in the past two days. Hunger and food hadn't crossed her mind. She hadn't needed any sleep either. She'd been reading around the clock without pause.

Ariana scanned through the library of works downloaded to her computer to choose what she would consume next. She flipped back through the history section and read the works of Josephus and Eusebius, then skipped forward and selected the complete works of H. P. Lovecraft to read afterwards.

She was settling in to continue when Esther came through the door. Ariana looked up for a moment, said nothing, and went back to reading. She processed that Esther didn't look well, but at that moment, she couldn't be imposed upon to actually care enough to do something helpful.

Esther shuffled over to Ariana. Her skin appeared almost jaundiced, and her eyes were held in a perpetual squint from the pain in her head. She shivered beneath three layers of clothes that she would likely take off again in the next fifteen minutes when she got too hot—for the fourth time in the last two hours.

"Where's Bryan?" she asked, speaking aloud as well as signing since Ariana hadn't looked up at her.

"Check the engine room," Ariana signed, still not looking at her. "He's probably there."

"He's not," Esther said, looking tired and defeated.

"Okay," Ariana said, staring at the screen of her computer. "Then check his room. Maybe he's sleeping or doing something else."

Esther slapped the desktop to get Ariana's attention.

"I checked his room too," Esther signed, hands moving through the air forcefully. "He's not there either."

"Well, then," Ariana signed with sharp, impatient movements to convey her own frustration, "I don't have a clue. Go ask Carlos."

Esther rolled her eyes and signed, "He doesn't know either. I just saw him in the hallway."

"I don't know what to tell you," Ariana blurted out, then signed the words after speaking. "Check with Morozov. Maybe she has him doing something. Hell, who knows, maybe those two are getting it on. There's a lot of that going around, if you haven't noticed."

Esther's nose wrinkled in disgust at the thought, but she could tell she'd get no further help from Ariana. She turned around and headed towards Morozov's quarters.

BRYAN

. . .

AFTER NOT EATING FOR TWO DAYS, BRYAN FELT JUST FINE. BETTER than fine, he felt like a new man. In just two days, his metabolism had kicked into high gear, as if attempting to reset his body to its original and optimal specs. His health issues cleared up. He felt energized, strong, and clearer minded than he had in years. The ship's workplace AI, Natalia, read articles to him in a Russian accent, discussing the latest developments in Quantum and Particle Physics. He multi-tasked by working out while he listened. He hadn't worked out in years. Not since the injuries and the diagnosis. He was always either too tired or in too much pain. He'd lost the drive over time.

But now it was back, and with his energy levels soaring, Bryan went from couch potato to beast mode in a matter of hours. The only time he stopped picking things up and putting them down was when he took a mental break and jumped on the VR gaming platform with the three-hundred-sixty-degree mobility. He loaded a military simulation game and continued getting exercise as he walked, ran, ducked, knelt, and ran some more, shooting enemies at every chance. For two days, he had remained wide awake, taking in no food while he continued to exercise, keeping his body in a state of constant caloric incineration. His metabolism was pushed to even higher limits by his thyroid kicking into hyperdrive for a short period of time.

In two days, Bryan lost thirty pounds while gaining a significant amount of muscle mass as well. It was amazing. He felt healthy. His skin wasn't sagging but was instead rebounding at a sufficient rate to stay tight and maintain elasticity. Where before he had a beer belly and the musculature of a man who did minimal manual labor for a living or otherwise, now his body was assuming a more powerful, thick-muscled frame, which in ages gone by would have been designed for crushing armored helms with a mace or cracking monkey skulls with polished thigh bones possessing vine wrapped handles for improved grip. Smart and capable of rallying men with a peculiar charisma, Bryan would have been a leader of some sort on the battlefield. Now, he didn't need to be such things, but he felt a drive to become more, to be all he could be, both physically and mentally. Brains and brawn. Engineer and aerospace nerd as well as the brute force and savage cunning of Conan the Barbarian.

Now all I need, he thought, *is a beautiful half-dressed woman lying at my feet, arms wrapped around one leg and ready to bed me.*

Bryan smiled, a big shit-eating grin, but it soon disappeared.

"Yeah," he grumbled, crestfallen, "in what universe?"

But Bryan's universe was different now. *He* was different. Different in ways he didn't yet understand. Possibly best he didn't understand.

He thought of Morozov. Envisioned her body naked and entangled with his own improved physique. Imagined the things they could do. On one hand, he admitted Esther and Ariana both were more attractive on pure looks alone, but Morozov had a hardness to her. She held an allure of mystery, danger, and strength that spoke directly to Bryan's lustful heart in ways the other women did not.

"I sense your arousal levels are peaking, Bryan," his personal AI Relaxation assistant said in a female voice. "Do you need me to activate erotic subroutines and project one of your preferred holovids?"

He thrust the thoughts of Morozov out of his head.

"No, Kim," Bryan said, annoyed. "I do not need your assistance at this time."

He went back to doing push-ups, squats, and lifting anything heavy he had on hand, wishing in that moment that he didn't have an implant transmitting physical data to Kim all the time. But he had saved his money and bought the top-of-the-line model. Full nervous system integration and activation. There were some options that involved physical accessories, but they weren't necessary to experience a full array of pleasurable feelings.

He made it another ten minutes before his thoughts returned to Morozov.

"Erotic subroutines activated," Kim said, as she appeared before him, her high-definition holographic projection manifested in all its sensual glory. Her flesh looked real. Supple. Soft but firm in all the right places. Her skin glistened with a light sheen of sweat that Bryan found so attractive. As if she were roaming the jungle in search of safety all day until she stumbled upon him, her savior. Just like Conan.

She dropped onto all fours and crawled across the floor to him.

"Your arousal levels crossed the preset threshold, Bryan," Kim said in a sultry voice as she wrapped both arms around one of his legs and pulled herself against him. She was immaterial, but the implant in his brain allowed her to fire off all the right nerves to give him the sensation of her body sliding against his, the pressure of her breasts parted by his lower thigh as she hugged him tightly and looked up to meet his gaze.

Bryan closed his eyes, wanting the pleasure of sexual sensations but wishing it wasn't this. He wished for the real thing.

"Do I have your permission to continue?" Kim asked.

He felt a pressure against his groin. He knew it was just nerve synapses firing, but it felt so real.

"Don't you want me?" Kim asked and rubbed her nipples back and forth over his leg. "Just say yes. Pleeeeaaase?"

Bryan enjoyed the sensations but didn't answer her yet.

"C'mon, baby, aren't you excited by me?" Kim asked. "It sure looks like you are." She tapped his erection with an index finger.

"Dammit, girl!" he said, looking down at her with excited frustration. "I'm harder than woodpecker lips right now! Geez!"

"I'm not complaining, baby," Kim said and kissed him through his pants. "Just say yes and let me work my magic."

Bryan was desperate for sex but drawn toward reality, not synthetic approximation, no matter how good it felt. He wanted to grip a real woman's hips and entangle his fingers in real hair.

"Baby, just tell me one thing," Kim said. "What would Conan do to me right now?"

"Oh my god," Bryan blurted out, shaking his head as his body quivered at the thought of the answer to her question. "Conan would throw you down on a pile of furs by a campfire and fuck the hell out of you right now! That's what Conan would do!"

"Then say yes and do it to me! Please, baby. Please?" Kim begged him in that breathy, desperate voice she was programmed for, her eyes big and brown and pleading with him as if she needed him like he needed oxygen. It was too much.

"Yes!" Bryan nearly growled the word.

"Mmmm," she said. "Good. And how do you want it, today?"

"Get on your knees, Kim," he answered, his tone low and urgent. "Activate the prosthetic. Maximize sensations." He undid the belt cinched around his waist, and the shorts fell without him even unzipping them. He pulled the underwear down as well and kicked both away from him.

The holo projection of Kim moved to the recliner chair and crawled up on the seat, her rear in the air, facing him. A panel opened on the side of the chair and a mechanical arm unfolded. A life-size synthetic replica of a woman's buttocks and genitals rose up and pivoted into place, merging with the holo projection so the synthetic masturbator wasn't even visible. He saw the holo projection of Kim's ass and sex and felt the solid synth flesh against his hands as he gripped her hips and pulled her to him, the holo projection matching his movements.

"Vaginal or anal entry?" Kim asked playfully.

"Vaginal," Bryan replied and entered her. Kim gasped and responded to his movements, keying off his actions and prior catalogued sessions to help her determine when she should take over and when she should receive, when to take control and when to give it up. This was a time to receive, she decided.

"You're lasting significantly longer than normal, Bryan," she said after some time. "I love it. Would you like to spank me, Bryan? Would you? C'mon, babe. Smack my ass. Hard!"

Bryan swung his open palm down like a hammer, and the contact resounded with a loud WHACK. It was hard enough it stung his palm only slightly when it should have hurt more.

"Again! Do it again, Bryan!"

Bryan swung harder this time. The sting was barely noticeable, and with each following slap, it diminished until he felt nothing.

Kim egged him on, recognizing the increase in his mental arousal. She continued talking dirty to him and begging him to spank her harder and harder, pushing him to experience increasingly more intense emotions and physical sensations until he was ready.

He drove his hips forward once more and locked them out. Kim knew it was time to take over, and she moved over him, grinding, squeezing, swirling, until he gasped and climaxed at last with a primal growl.

He was sweating like he'd run a marathon. Bryan looked at the clock and realized he'd gotten lost in the moment. He'd been pounding Kim at a steady pace nonstop for just under an hour.

This is not normal, he thought, *but holy shit it's awesome!*

He looked down. He was hard and standing at attention.

"Hot damn! You're still ready to fight for God and country, aren't ya, boy." Bryan laughed at his joke while feeling quite pleased with his performance and stamina. He needed a shower, though. Bryan thanked Kim for a good time and walked off to the shower while she saw to the cleaning and storage of the prosthetic device.

Bryan finished his shower and was just toweling dry when he heard a knock at his door.

"Captain Morozov is here," Kim notified him.

He looked at his figure in the mirror again. He felt confident for the first time in years. He was still a large man, but he looked solid and strong. Like an ox. *A sexy-ass ox*, he thought.

He wrapped the towel around his waist and walked to the exit.

Morozov

. . .

MOROZOV CONFINED HERSELF TO HER QUARTERS AFTER THEY SET course for the source of the signal. She wasn't sure why she did it. She just knew she needed time to herself. Time to metamorphose was the vague feeling she got. Her quarters felt like a cocoon. She was a butterfly preparing to emerge. But she wasn't soft. She was an iron, razor-winged butterfly forged in the fire of experience and polished with the knowledge of those who came before her.

She spent her time reading military biographies, accounts of leaders, military strategy, principles of leadership shared throughout the ages. She consumed books retelling the stories of great battles. Julius Caesar, Hannibal, Xenophon and his Ten Thousand, the Spartans at Thermopylae, Napoleon, and more, right up through the reclaiming of Mars from the scavengers two decades before.

Morozov also noticed her body changing. Her legs were fitter, her thighs and calves more muscular. The muscles of her arms and back and her abs stood out, visible at a glance, even beneath her clothes. The scar on her face had faded even as the line of her jaw sharpened, and her skin was soft and supple to the touch, nearly glowing with a radiance she had never experienced before, even after occasional bouts of great sex.

Her eyes were one of the most noticeable changes. They had transformed into a deeper, piercing shade of blue that played off her golden blonde hair to dramatically improve her sex appeal and sense of mystery. Her hair had grown long in the last two days as well. From almost a short buzz cut to shoulder length. She had noticed the rate of growth in passing but thought nothing of it until she began to feel it tickling at her face and neck.

Staring into the mirror now, she assessed her overall appearance, and what she saw was exactly what she had always dreamed she would become.

Hard as steel but beautiful and soft … and sexy. Sensual and sexy, but smart, tactically brilliant, and possessing a titanium backbone. Someone worthy of respect and honor and yet someone to be desired and loved. She wanted it all. But first …

She put her tablet down and closed the screen. A torrent of hormones coursed through her system, flooding her body with physical desire as her mind turned toward thoughts of being wanted, being lusted after. She longed to fulfill and be fulfilled. To please and be pleased. To be the object of lust, a bearer of sultry glory hot enough to burn the heart of any man or woman. She longed to submit and dominate. To be plowed and to ride. To lose control and take control.

Morozov considered her options. Carlos was a no go. Handsome as he was, he was scared of her, and she couldn't respect that. Ariana or Miko might suffice, but they, too, were frightened by her in their own ways. Esther. Esther was too fragile right now, even though she admired the young woman immensely.

Bryan.

He wasn't particularly handsome, but she found him funny, entertaining, and he wasn't afraid of her. He'd spoken with her on many an occasion, sharing his honest opinions whether she liked them or not. She could trust him to be honest with her if nothing else.

Staring in the mirror, Morozov told herself that even two days ago, she would have been a worthy catch for Bryan, still above his league … but now, she was magnificent. She was desirable above the masses. He wouldn't turn her down. He would not simply accept her proposition, he would leap at the opportunity and seek to ravish her body. He would devour her and she him.

In the shower, she sang songs of love and steamy sex as she washed away the grime of the last few days. When she dried her hair, it fell to her shoulders in wavy golden locks without any attempt to fix it. She slipped on black yoga pants and a white midriff shirt with no sleeves. Her nipples pushed through the fabric, and her breasts, which had always been a large C-cup, stood high and held tight like never before. She grabbed a bottle of vodka and a bottle of whiskey and set off for Bryan's room, sauntering through the hallways, hips swaying like a big cat as she walked, her steps light and controlled, her posture communicating danger, confidence, and sexual hunger.

She reached Bryan's quarters and knocked.

He opened the door with only a towel wrapped around his waist to cover his body. She immediately noted the improvements in his physical form. Loss of fat, additional muscle, and muscles that were far more toned and bulging than before. He was solid. A powerlifter build made to carry, build, and fight.

She bit her bottom lip unconsciously for a second, then spoke.

"Wow," she said, "you've ... changed."

Bryan looked Morozov up and down, lips pressed tight and shifting against one another. His eyebrows stood at attention.

"Damn, boss," Bryan said. "So have you."

Morozov smiled as he continued to stare at her, starting back over at the top.

"Your eyes ... they're so much bluer now ... and the long blonde hair is right damn sexy ... and your tits. Jesus Christ! They were fantastic before, but now they look like they're prepared to launch a missile attack on me eyes. Mmm, mmm, mmm."

Morozov spun in a circle slowly so he could see her backside.

"Goddamn, woman ... you had an awesome ass before, but you could bounce a stack of quarters off those glutes now. I bet they'd rebound off the damn ceiling and put an eye out."

Morozov chuckled. "Well, Bryan, crass as ever, but that's part of what I've always liked about you. You've never tried to be something you weren't, and what you are, I find entertaining. So, there's no sense in pretending we don't want to fuck like rabbits. You obviously like what you see, and so do I." She glanced down at his member lifting the towel as it stood to attention.

Bryan looked down, then back at her and grinned. "He knows a good thing when he sees it, ma'am." Bryan winked and nodded.

"Okay then," Morozov said, "I have a proposition. I have vodka and whiskey to share ... but *only* if you join me in *my* quarters. What say you, sir?"

"I say mission accepted. My partner and I are ready to deploy at a moment's notice, no matter how dangerous the mission may be."

"Dangerous?" Morozov asked, one eyebrow cocked.

"Yeah, boss," Bryan replied, "if your ass is any indication, that pussy of yours has probably grown muscles on top of muscles. You might break us." He said the last sentence in his best imitation of a Russian accent.

Morozov almost dropped the bottle of whiskey as she laughed so hard it bent her over.

"Goddammit, Bryan," she said, trying to stop laughing and wiping the tears from her eyes with the back of one hand. "C'mon. We have a *long* night ahead of us."

"Sounds grand, boss," he said, "but, technically, it's only early afternoon."

Morozov looked at him, straight faced. "I know," she said and turned away.

"All-righty then! Let me just grab some clothes real quick."

"Don't bother," Morozov called over her shoulder.

Bryan's eyes widened. "Right on," he muttered under his breath and hurried after her.

CARLOS

CARLOS'S IDEA OF PARADISE WAS NAKED WOMEN AND SEX ALL DAY AND night.

And it showed. In two days, he'd had sex with Miko three times and practically begged Ariana three times to have sex with him. If he hadn't known Esther was sick and out of commission, he'd have approached her as well.

Morozov wasn't even an option, though, so it just left Miko. But

Miko wasn't feeling the same level of drive and desire he was. He needed to watch it, do it, embed it in his mind. He needed to surround himself with sex and nothing else.

If he had any clue what kind of high-tech toy Bryan had in his room, he would have begged to use the holo projector and prosthetic attachments non-stop.

He was a pilot. A hot shot. The cool guy. He had nearly been a regular chiseled Adonis before, but now he embodied the term. Skin bronze and muscles cut and ripped.

My dick is bigger too, man, he thought as he looked at his naked body in the mirror. *I could be a fucking porn star now, if I wanted. I'd have girls dying to fuck me whether they got paid or not.*

He hit play on the porn video, and it filled the TV screen covering one wall of his quarters. At this rate, his stash of lube was not going to last the whole trip. Hell, if he kept jerking off this many times a day, it wouldn't last a week.

He didn't care, though. He had to do it again. The desire and drive were too much to ignore. The tingling sensations in the upper shaft of his penis were so strong he couldn't keep his hips still, and he kept flexing his Kegel muscles over and over uncontrollably. It was annoying and even painful at times.

He needed a release. A break from those feelings.

He jerked off again and climaxed. The escape didn't last long. He needed a woman. A real woman. He needed Miko. He cleaned up, dressed, and headed out to find her. Beg her to fuck him. He needed it. God, he needed it.

Carlos hurried down the hallway toward Miko's office. Halfway there, he bumped into Esther.

"Ho, girl!" Carlos said as Esther bounced off his chest after rounding the corner without looking. "What's the rush?"

Esther apologized. "I'm sorry," she signed and said. "I'm trying to find Bryan. Have you seen him?"

"Bryan, huh?" Carlos asked, a suspicious look crinkling his face with lines. "What you need him for? Can't I help meet your needs?"

Esther's head was pounding. Her body was aching and tired and felt much like someone was hitting her with little hammers all over with every second the signal continued to broadcast. She was oblivious to Carlos's come on.

"What?" Esther asked. "I don't know. I want to get some of the rubber flooring to put in my room. If Bryan can't point me to some extra in storage, I'm going to rip up the engine room floor to get what I need! So, can you help me with that?"

Carlos's eyes squinted as his cheeks drew up and nostrils flared in disgust.

"No," he said. "I have no idea. I'm a fucking pilot, not the janitor. And no, I don't know where he's at either. Maybe him and Morozov are fucking."

Esther did a double take at Carlos, staring at the back of his head as he moved down the hall toward Medical, where Miko was likely working.

"What the fuck is up with y'all thinking Morozov and Bryan are fucking?" she said aloud, but Carlos ignored her and kept walking.

He reached Medical, knocked on the door, and entered. Miko was sitting at a table inspecting her thumb. She didn't acknowledge him. He folded down the waistband of his workout shorts so they rode right at the top of his pubic bone, showing off his lower abs and lack of underwear while being shirtless showed off his chest and midsection. He was acting like any colorful male animal would when trying to mate, flashing his best physical attributes to attract the female's attention. He moved toward her, upper torso swaying side to side like a snake, head down, eyes up, trying to act old school gangster, hoping it came off as a mixture of sexy and tough.

"Hey, girl," he said when she still didn't notice him, "you want to take another ride on this bull? If you're hungry, I can fill you up. You know what I'm sayin'?"

Carlos had moved all the way up to the table Miko sat at. It was a narrow portion extending off of her main desk. He pressed his thighs against the edge of the desktop, his genitals thrust over the edge toward her.

Without a word or a glance up from her left thumb, Miko picked up the scalpel and performed a backhand slash incision in a single wickedly fast movement. No sooner was it complete then she sat the scalpel down and started the timer.

Carlos didn't even feel the cut at first. Didn't realize what she had done for maybe three seconds. But then he looked down and saw the red line parting the flesh just above his shorts. Probably between six to eight inches across. Saw the blood begin to run and his intestines partially protrude through the opening in his abdominal wall.

His hands instinctively reached down and pressed against the wound, trying to hold his bowels inside his body.

"*What the fuck?!?*" Carlos yelled out, staggering back. Miko stared intently at the area his hands were covering. "What the fuck is wrong with you? You fucking bitch! Why'd you do that to me?"

"Goddammit, Carlos," Miko said, annoyed. "You're fucking this up. Come over here and lay on my exam table. I need to watch and record what happens."

She stood and walked around the desk towards him. Carlos staggered back a step, fear and shock in his eyes.

"Look, you idiot," she told him, "I'm conducting an experiment. I sliced my thumb to the bone an hour ago and now it's like I never did it." She held up her left thumb. "So, lay down on the table and let's see how fast you heal. Our bodies are capable of crazy stuff now."

She maneuvered around behind Carlos and pushed him toward the exam table.

"Don't you think you could have warned me?" he exclaimed, trying to glance over his shoulder as she moved him across the room. "You know, given me a heads up and got me on board first? Huh?"

"Ummm ..." Miko hesitated. "Okay ... I guess so ... Yeah. I was just pretty focused on finding out ... you know?" She turned him around and issued a voice command to the table. "Table lower eight inches." The table dropped down, and she pushed him into a seated position.

He looked her in the eye. "Dammit, Miko," he said, "you gotta get someone's permission before you cut them. For fuck's sake."

"Jesus Christ, Carlos," Miko said as she turned him and lifted his legs up onto the exam table. "I thought you were some gung-ho tough boy pilot. Don't be such a pussy. You're going to be perfectly fine. It's just a matter of how many minutes it takes for your body to heal up."

She looked at the timer.

"We're already at the two-minute mark," she informed him as she grabbed a stack of sterilized gauze pads. "Now move your hands and let me see."

Carlos reluctantly removed them, looking at the wound as he did so. He was shocked to see it had stopped bleeding already.

"Holy shit, man," Miko said. "You're healing up faster than I did. No bleeding, and it appears your guts are pulling back and aligning themselves internally. I can see the peritoneum membrane reconnecting to hold your organs in place!"

Carlos lay there, and Miko pulled up a chair, positioning the table height where she could see down into the wound with ease. Fifteen minutes after injury and the muscles of Carlos's abdominal wall had knit themselves back together. Ten minutes later and his skin was healthy and pink without a scar.

"Wow," she said. "You just healed up in twenty-five minutes from an eviscerating injury! Do you know how crazy that is? And there isn't even a scar to tell it happened."

Carlos smiled at the newfound ability of his body. He was a certifiable badass. Damn near Wolverine level badass. Sans claws, of course, but that didn't matter to him. His wandering mind returned to how this all started, though, and his smoldering anger flared back up. He was still pissed with Miko for just cutting him without warning or asking him to volunteer to participate in the experiment.

That's fucked up, he thought again.

However, at the same time, he was glad to have learned this incredible information about his body. It was amazing.

Miko rubbed a finger over the place the wound had been, then grabbed a cloth, wet it, and wiped off the dried blood. He tried to get visibly angry but couldn't manage it. A part of him thought her actions were somehow sexy, even though he couldn't make it make sense. And now that she was touching him, his body was getting alarmingly aroused.

"That's fucking hot," Miko told Carlos as she traced her finger over his newly repaired skin.

A look passed between them. She snatched his shoes off, then jerked his shorts down, pulled them off, and tossed them across the room. She knelt on the table.

"Take me," she said, her voice low and husky. "Take me now."

She didn't have to tell Carlos again.

ESTHER

FRUSTRATED DIDN'T BEGIN TO EXPRESS HOW ESTHER FELT AT THIS point. For three days now, she had felt like shit. Physically, emotionally, mentally. You name it, it felt like shit. But no one on the ship gave a damn. None of them cared. They might as well have been zombie slaves or hypnotized servants answering the call of their master. They were all hell bound and determined to reach the source of the signal, and nothing else mattered. Period. No thing and no one. Not one fuck was given about Esther suffering every minute. Didn't matter to them one bit.

And now that she had decided to try out a potential solution to help her out, Bryan was nowhere to be found and Ariana couldn't be bothered to help her find him and neither could Carlos. He was headed to see Miko.

Esther seriously doubted Miko knew, and she had a feeling what

Carlos was going there for also. There was no way she was going to follow behind him right now.

And what the hell is up with both Ariana and Carlos anyway? She thought. *Both of them suggested that Bryan and Morozov might be screwing each other. What the fuck? Ugh! One, it's gross! But two, why are they assuming everyone on board is focused on sex so much? Particularly, those two. They're as different as night and day. I can't even imagine them hooking up. Might as well try to make oil and water mix.*

Esther didn't understand, and honestly, she didn't want to understand. She just wanted some goddamn relief. A bit of respite from this pounding sensation in her body and head.

She continued toward Morozov's quarters. When she arrived, Esther pressed the call button. She waited several seconds, then pressed it again. This time she waited half a minute. Still no answer.

Esther groaned and closed her eyes, beyond frustrated, but then she had a gut feeling that she might not want to push this any further. Her desire for relief overrode her intuition, however. She selected the press-to-talk button and spoke out loud.

"Captain Morozov, it's Esther."

She released the button and waited. A few seconds later, Morozov's face appeared. At least, it looked like Morozov ... mostly. The hair was noticeably different at once, and her eyes. But there was something more about her cheeks and jaws that looked different.

Is she wearing a wig and colored contact lenses? Esther thought. *Maybe some kind of makeup altering the lines of her face slightly? And what's she rocking back and forth for?*

"Give me a minute," Morozov signed. Sweat beaded on her brow, and a few droplets cast off from her fingers as her hands moved.

The camera feed closed. If Esther could hear, she would have heard the loud sounds emanating from Morozov's quarters as Bryan and Morozov brought each other to a life altering climax, something so intense, neither had ever experienced anything like it before. Morozov climbed off of him when her legs stopped shaking enough to support her once again, then walked over to her closet and grabbed shorts and a long T-shirt. Bryan rolled off the bed, lit a cigar, and stuck it in his mouth, then wrapped the towel around his waist and strolled to the door. He slapped the pressure plate, and the doors parted.

Esther's eyes grew big as her chin tucked and her head tried to retreat right off her shoulders. She took two steps back, then looked at the floor.

Who the hell is that? Esther thought. *And how did he get on board?*

"What in the world is wrong with you, kid?" Bryan asked, then realized Esther wasn't looking at his lips. He made sure the towel was tucked in on itself and secure about his waist before letting go of it. He reached out and snapped his fingers in her line of sight. Esther looked up, and Bryan repeated himself, verbally and by signing.

"What in the world is wrong with you, kid? Hmm? Cat got your tongue? Fingers in a knot?"

Esther stared at Bryan, not recognizing him. Her brain couldn't rationally suspect that he was capable of changing his appearance so dramatically in two days. To her, he was a stranger.

"Goddamn, girl," Bryan said. "I ain't the Ghost of Christmas Future come to recount your sins and tell of your pending death. I mean, geez. I know I look different, but you look about as confused as a fart in a fan factory."

He inhaled on the cigar and blew the smoke out, angling it upward with his bottom lip.

"Bryan?" Esther asked, speaking the word as she signed his name slowly, head leaning forward and one eye squinting.

"The one and only," he said and smiled. "Whaddaya think, huh?" He looked down at his body as he asked. "This damn signal is something else. I've never looked or felt better in my entire life."

Esther shook her head in disbelief. "You look great," she said, "but can you put on some clothes? I need your help."

"Hmph," Bryan grunted. "I don't presently have any at my disposal. Captain needed my *services* in a hurry, if you get my drift." He tilted his head and cocked an eyebrow when he said the word services.

Esther's stomach turned.

"To much information, Bryan," she signed to him. "Will you please go get some clothes from your room and help me out?"

He puffed on the cigar once again and leaned on the doorway.

"What exactly do you need help with?" he asked.

"I want some of the rubberized floormats," Esther told him. "I want to line the walls of my room with them and then roll up in them to sleep. Try and soundproof my room enough it cuts down on the vibrations from the signal. At this point, any amount of improvement is worth the effort."

Bryan nodded in understanding.

"I gotcha. Yeah, I can help you out. Meet me at the engine room in ten minutes," he told her.

Morozov walked up just then and signed, "Hello, Esther."

Esther signed, "Hello, Captain," in response.

"Esther here," Bryan said, "needs my help. She's decided it's time to soundproof her room with some rubber floormats and reduce the vibrations, like we discussed a few days ago. I'm gonna get dressed and help her."

Bryan gave a mock salute to Morozov and went to walk away. Morozov slapped his ass.

"Good game, Bryan," she said. "When you're done, make sure you come back so we can pick up where we left off."

"Oh, don't you worry, Captain," Bryan said. "Imma butter both sides of your biscuit before we're done tonight." Bryan winked at her, then stuck the cigar back in his mouth and walked off.

Esther was still cringing when she looked back at Morozov.

"Well, Captain," she signed, "I guess I'll see you later."

Without waiting for a response, Esther turned and walked straight to the engine room. Ten minutes later, Bryan met her there.

"All right, short stuff," Bryan signed, cigar still in his mouth. "You want rubber floormats, right?"

Esther nodded.

"Okay," Bryan replied. "Follow me."

He led her out of the engine room, hung a right, and another right, then a left, and they entered the bay area where the Daddy Long Leg bots were kept when not in use.

"Jackpot!" Bryan said, turning to face Esther with arms spread and palms upturned. "The whole floor here is covered with the rubber matting. Let's get to work and pull it up."

Bryan dove right in, while Esther did what she could. Bending over was killing her head, but she refused to just sit down and let Bryan do all the work. When they had stacked all the rubber floor mats in one place, except for the few directly under the Daddy Long Legs, Bryan spoke up.

"We're gonna need tape as well," he said, "to hang them on the walls and make them stick together. I'll grab some." Bryan walked away and returned with two rolls of reinforced, high tensile strength tape. "Okay, girl," he said. "I think we're done. You take the tape and a small stack of these, and I'll grab as much as I can carry." Bryan hefted the stack and pressed it overhead before lowering it onto the crown of his skull, using both hands to keep it balanced. "After you," Bryan indicated cutting his eyes and tilting his head slightly. Esther nodded and moved out.

It took them three trips to shuttle them all to her room. Afterwards, Bryan and Esther worked side by side to cover the walls of her quarters and tape everything in place.

"There you go," Bryan said, smiling. "And we have plenty left over." He pointed at the remaining squares.

Esther bent the fingers of her right hand ninety degrees at the first knuckles then raised it just above her head and moved it back and forth.

Bryan looked incredulous.

"Ceiling?" he asked. "You want to cover the ceiling too?"

Esther nodded and signed "Yes."

The ceiling would be a little tricky. There were two light fixtures, and he would need to cut out holes just big enough to fit over them.

Bryan sighed and ran a hand through his hair. "All right, short stuff, you just standby and hand me tape or mat squares when I need them."

Esther nodded in agreement. Bryan took the matt squares from her and taped them to the ceiling in all the places that wouldn't overlap the light fixtures. Once he had those in place, he determined where he would have to cut to fit the mat squares as snugly as possible around the fixtures.

He sat down to cut the squares and marveled at the realization that his neck was not bothering him at all. Even in his youth, looking up and working with things overhead for so long without a break would have him majorly sore and stiff. But he felt fine. No issues of any kind.

Crazy, he thought and chuckled to himself.

Esther noticed the slight smile on his face and the jiggling of his chest as he laughed lightly. "What's funny?" she signed and said.

"Oh," Bryan looked up at her. "Just realized my neck isn't sore after doing this." He pointed at the ceiling. "These changes in my body ... they've been wild and weird, and by weird, I mean nuttier than a squirrel turd."

Esther's nose and eyebrows wrinkled up in confusion. "Huh?" she said and signed.

"You know," he said. "Crazy ... basically. I'm still noticing little things too. Just strikes me as odd all over again each time I notice something new."

"Gotcha," Esther replied.

Bryan took a drag off his cigar and paused from cutting the rubber mat.

"You know, Esther," he said, "I'm truly sorry you're not experiencing all the wonderful things we are, and I'm even more sorry that the signal is hurting you."

Esther looked Bryan in the eye, her brow furrowed. "Not sorry enough to vote 'No' to going there, though."

Bryan shifted his closed lips to one side and nodded. "True," he admitted. "But," and he held up an index finger, "I *do* care enough to help you do this—because I could be banging Morozov's ass like a salvation army drum right now!" He laughed hard. "Instead, I'm helping you, but it's okay. I'll still get to do that here in a little while."

Bryan grinned big and went back to cutting out the mats to fit. His spatial awareness was quite good before, but now it was amazingly accurate. He put the pieces in place and taped them down. They fit perfectly.

"Okay, then," Bryan said, assessing their work. "I believe you are set! Anything else I can help with before I leave?" he asked Esther.

"No," she replied, her index and middle finger tapping against her thumb twice like a mouth opening and closing. "I can tape these others together to wrap myself up in."

"Roger that," he acknowledged and headed for the door. "I hope it helps, girl." With that, he walked out the door and headed back towards Morozov's quarters.

Esther taped together enough squares to roll herself up in, covering above the crown of her head to below her feet. Once done, she placed them on the floor, swallowed a sleep aid and muscle relaxer, then laid on one end, held on, and rolled toward the other end, cocooning herself up like the proverbial bug in a rug at the foot of the bunk beds. Ariana would just have to climb over her.

She sighed long and gentle as she felt the difference the mats made. It was significant. The vibrations were nowhere near as strong. For the first time in over two days, Esther slept a deep, restful sleep.

5

Four Days Travelled Toward the Signal

MIKO HAD SPENT THE LAST TWO DAYS BRIBING CARLOS WITH ONE sexual act after another to be her guinea pig and let her injure him and record how long it took him to heal. She assured him the pain he experienced would pale in comparison to the pleasure she rewarded him with.

Carlos, being entirely driven by his sexual desires, agreed.

Miko took a methodical approach, measuring the length and depth of incisions and gradually increasing both. She cut through the thigh muscles, calves, glutes, back, and biceps. Once, after telling Carlos she was going to make a deeper incision in his calf muscle and he laid face down on the exam table, she switched targets and slashed through his Achilles tendon. He threw his head back and raised up on his forearms without even thinking.

"You *lying* bitch!" he cursed her, then proceeded to clench his teeth and growl like a wounded animal ready to attack.

"Aaahhh, it's okay," she said. "You know by now it's going to heal. Just a matter of how long it takes."

"*Goddammit, Miko,*" Carlos growled, jaw still clenched. "*I swear, I'm gonna make you choke on my cock for that one.*"

"Ha! You wish," Miko fired back. "Haven't you noticed? I don't have a gag reflex anymore. I got rid of it." A smug smile spread across her face as she cocked one eyebrow and tilted her chin up in challenge.

"Well then, we'll just have to see how long you can go without air before you pass out," Carlos countered, determined to get his revenge.

He grew quiet for several seconds, and then the meaning of Miko's words clicked, and Carlos finally grasped the idea she had conveyed.

"'Hold on," he said. "What did you say about your gag reflex? You *got rid of it?* What the hell do you mean, 'got rid of it?'"

Miko shrugged. "I don't know," she said. "Just what I said. I decided I didn't want one, so I told my body to get rid of it ... and it did."

"Just like that?" Carlos asked, incredulous.

"Yeah. Just like that. Same way I made my tongue longer and my tits a little bigger." She stuck her tongue out, the tip extending down to wrap under her chin, and placed her hands under both breasts to emphasize the larger cup size and how heavy and full they were. "Haven't you noticed?" She now sounded irritated. Offended. She wanted to cut him again, but this time without any thought of experimentation. She almost did, but he spoke first and smoothed things over.

"Yeah, I noticed," he said. "I just figured it happened on its own. I had no idea you could make your body change however you want it to. That's ... that's crazy."

"Isn't it?" Miko asked in agreement, forgetting the imagined slight already. "I have to think about what else I might want to alter for the sake of experimentation and then try it."

Carlos laid his chin on his forearms and grinned.

"I know exactly what I'm going to focus on and change. I'm

going to concentrate on making my cock bigger," Carlos said. "See if it works."

Miko slapped his ass, and they both laughed.

"Guys," she said. "It never fails, never changes. All of you want a bigger cock."

She looked down and watched as the final tissues along Carlos's Achilles tendon knitted together and his body was whole again.

"Wow!" Miko exclaimed. "It only took you thirteen minutes to completely heal a severed Achilles tendon."

Carlos sat up on the table, then slipped down and put his feet on the floor, testing the strength of the tendon. He put all his weight on it, then bounced a little, and finally took off at a sprint for four steps, then stopped, turned around, and repeated the movement.

"Damn! It feels perfectly fine."

"Okay," Miko said, "I have a proposition for our next test. I'll pre-set a tourniquet around the crook of your leg just in case we need to use it. Then we'll slice your femoral artery open and see how quickly you stop bleeding."

"Hmmm, no," Carlos said. "Your turn. We put the tourniquet on your leg, you show me where to cut, and I'll slice *your* femoral artery open."

"Really?" Miko said, cocking an eyebrow and tilting her head down as she stared at him. It didn't have the affect she was hoping for.

"Oh yeah. Really." Carlos's mind was made up.

"Okay, okay," she said, raising her hands in surrender.

Miko grabbed a tourniquet and sat on the exam table. She slipped her foot through the tourniquet, slid it up to the crook of her hip, then extended her leg out straight. Carlos picked up the scalpel and walked around to her right side. He leaned over slightly, looking at her inner thigh.

"Where do I stick ya?" he asked, his excitement a little unnerving to Miko now that the shoe was on the other foot.

She pointed to where the femoral artery could be reached midway down her inner thigh. Carlos stabbed the scalpel into

Miko's leg without warning, exactly where she had just pointed. Once it was inside, he cut upward toward the front of her thigh, creating a deep incision easily four inches long.

Miko sucked in air in surprise, but she didn't scream. She hardly felt any pain. Carlos started the clock and looked at Miko, a big shit-eating grin plastered over his face. Miko's eyebrows bunched up in a line of deep furrow, and she gave him a *What the fuck?* look.

Carlos shrugged and said, "Oh, I'm sorry. Did I surprise you?" He smiled and winked at her.

"Bastard," she said and looked down at the wound. The flow of blood pumping out of her femoral artery was already slowing. Within one minute, it was only a light steady flow, and by the two-minute mark, all bleeding had ceased. She never once felt light-headed or broke out in a cold sweat. Eighteen minutes later, Miko was perfectly healed.

"Okay," Carlos said. "I get to pick a test this time."

Miko didn't trust Carlos at this point any more than he trusted her; however, she had a test in mind she wanted to perform but didn't think he would agree to unless she could make a deal without telling him.

"Okay," Miko agreed, "but the last test I get to choose, and you're my guinea pig."

Carlos's lower lip rose up in the middle, and he bobbed his head side to side, weighing the offer.

"All right," he said. "You got a deal."

Carlos walked over to a cabinet, opened it up, and reached down on the bottom shelf. There was a small square-head hammer with a rubber coating lying there. He picked it up and hefted it, getting a feel for its weight.

"C'mere," he said to Miko, and curled the index finger of his free hand, inviting her over.

She walked over to where he stood at her desk.

"Lay your hand on the table and spread your fingers wide."

Miko's breath caught in her throat. *Broken bones.* They hadn't tried that yet. An image of her hand being smashed popped into her mind, and she shivered. She made herself place her left hand down on the table and tried to focus on the knowledge they were gaining through these experiments and not the injury to come.

How bad can it hurt? she thought, trying to diminish her fear. *I barely felt the deep muscle cut in my thigh.*

She spread her fingers.

Carlos reached down and pinched the tip of her index finger, then wiggled it back and forth.

"What's that old nursery rhyme?" he asked. "This little piggy, right? Yeah, that's right. So, this little piggy right here, this one went to the market to buy some food." He let go and pinched the tip of her middle finger and wiggled it. "And this little piggy ... well, we both know what you use this little piggy for." Carlos gave her a dirty grin and chuckled, then moved on to pinch the tip of her ring finger. "This little piggy went to the bar looking for a ring." Carlos stuck out his tongue at Miko.

"Fat fucking chance," she said, "you little shit."

Carlos kept smiling and moved on to her pinky finger. Miko had a moment of butterflies fluttering around in her stomach. It was either going to be her pinky or her thumb. She didn't look forward to either one.

"And this little piggy ..." Carlos said, pinching the fingertip and wiggling the finger for only a moment before letting it go and swinging the hammer down with all his strength. As the hammer struck its target, Carlos yelled, "And this little piggy got its fucking skull bashed in and went wee wee wee all the way home, leaving a trail of blood and brains behind it."

The impact shattered the bone of Miko's fingertip into dozens of splinters and shards while simultaneously crushing over three thousand nerve receptors. Pain flared like a supernova. Before the signal, she would have blacked out. No question about it. But now? She showed a modicum of pain, but she didn't scream; she maintained her composure.

"Moth-er-fuck-er!" She half growled. "God damn, that hurts."

She breathed deep and blew out slowly through her nose, controlling her breath completely.

Within a minute, the pain was fading and her body was repairing itself. Bone shards knit themselves back together as the mashed marrow reorganized itself within the puzzle pieces, reassembling her fingertip. Splattered flesh grew back in place. The nailbed reattached while the mangled nail fell off and a new one began to grow. In a little under ten minutes, the outside was whole and normal looking, but she could feel the bone as it finished knitting itself back together.

Twenty minutes. That's all it took.

"Impressive," Carlos said. "And I don't just mean how quickly you healed. Impressive control with that level of pain."

Miko nodded. "Thanks. I'd have passed right out and woke up screaming if that had happened to me before the signal. This is crazy stuff."

Rubbing her fingertip, Miko walked over to a different cabinet and retrieved the laser scalpel. She dialed it to the max power and length, four inches, checked it, then turned it off and slid it in her pocket, angling her body so Carlos wouldn't see her do it. She then acted as if she put the item back and looked around further as if she couldn't find what she really wanted. She sighed and shut the door, then walked back over to Carlos, hands in her pockets.

"Your turn," she said bluntly. "Left hand on the table, fingers spread." She palmed the laser scalpel with a relaxed hand, pulled it out, and held it down by her leg.

"Okay," Carlos said. He placed his hand on the table and spread his fingers as instructed. "Now what do you want to do?" he asked her.

"Close your eyes," Miko said, acting coy.

"Fuck no!" he said.

"Will you close them while I grab what I need?" She fluttered her eyelashes at him.

"Hell fuck-ing no!" Carlos announced to Miko loudly, throwing his head back, chin in the air.

Miko seized the moment, pressing the button to turn the laser scalpel on as she brought her hand up and swung it down in one continuous stroke. The laser struck the table, cutting partially into the surface. Next to the lacerated surface, the tips of Carlos's index, middle, and ring fingers lay separated from his hand.

Carlos looked down and screamed.

"You fucking bitch! You sneaky, cock sucking bitch! You cut off my fingers! My fucking fingers!"

He raised his hand and gripped it around the wrist as he stared at it, the cauterized stumps smoldering before his eyes, the smell of his own burnt flesh filling his nostrils.

"Fucking hell! What is wrong with you, you lying bitch? You cut off my fucking fingers! And not just one! *NOOOOOO! THREEEEE!*" He folded his pinky finger in and trapped it with his thumb and held up the three finger stumps for emphasis. "*THREE* fucking fingers!" He shook his head. "Goddamn you, woman! All you want is the data. Isn't it?" Carlos didn't wait for her to answer. "I know it is. You selfish bitch. You don't even know whether they'll grow back. Just because we can heal tissue, what makes you think I can regrow severed bones? Huh?"

Miko stood with the laser scalpel held down by her leg again, eyes tracking Carlos's hand like a bird of prey does a field mouse as he moved it all around, vigilantly watching and waiting for the experiment's results.

"Oh, for fuck's sake!" he yelled when she didn't answer and instead only kept staring at his hand. "You want to see them so bad? Fuck it! Take a close look!"

He shoved his finger stumps in her face. Miko moved her head back and focused on the severed ends. Her mouth formed an O for a moment.

"Look at them, Carlos!" she said, excitement electrifying her voice and face. "They're growing back. They're fucking growing back!"

Carlos twisted his hand to look straight on at the ends of his fingers. He saw white bone sprouting from each of the stumps, and dark red tissue snaked up around the new growth.

Holy shit, he thought. *She's right.*

He extended his fingers and spread them and held his hand up level with his face, palm facing away. He watched silently as his body regenerated the severed digits. Bone finished forming; muscle and tendon extended and attached. Skin grew to cover each of the three fingertips, then the nailbeds formed and produced fingernails.

Crazy, man, he thought and shook his head. *This is absolutely fucking crazy.* Carlos watched in simultaneous disbelief and awe as the regeneration process concluded. He turned his hand about, looking at it from different angles.

"Woah!" Miko said loudly. "You're healing even faster than me. That only took you twelve minutes! Oh my God. I wonder … are you healing quicker the more you get injured? I mean, is your body adapting to repeated injury by increasing the rate at which it heals?"

Miko was in awe of the possibilities.

Carlos turned and looked at her, eyes wide, face a bit slack, still unable to fathom just how this could all be real and what it would mean for them going forward.

"What the fuck are we now, Miko? *Goddamn lizards*? Did that signal activate our reptilian brain or something? Is *that* how my body could do this?"

Miko shook her head side to side slowly, eyebrows arched high on her forehead.

"I have no friggin clue," she confessed. "But holy shit, man. You gotta admit, this is friggin awesome!"

She ran her hands through her hair as her eyes scanned the floor, looking for nothing in particular. She looked up and snapped her fingers.

"Okay," she said. "We gotta do another test." Before Carlos could object, Miko just blurted out her request. "Punch me."

"What?" Carlos said sharply, his tone high pitched, his face scrunched up in confusion. "Punch you?"

"Yes. Punch me. Punch me in the fucking jaw. Hard."

She squinted with determination as she braced herself for the impact, chin tucked, neck muscles rigid, jaw clenched.

"For real?"

Miko pointed at the left side of her jaw. "Hit me, bitch. Unless you're scared that I'll eat it like a champ and make you look like a punk." Miko grinned and sneered at Carlos, both nostrils flaring out and upward.

"Oh, hell no, you didn't."

Carlos planted his right foot, drew his right hand back almost to left field, and let rip an arcing hook punch, striking Miko right on the button where jaw and chin meet. There was a loud cracking sound, and her head snapped as if it were on a swivel. Her body spun, and Miko lost her balance. She fell but landed on her hands and knees, catching herself. Her head swung side to side, wobbling on her neck, cheeks flapping, then she jumped back up to her feet and faced Carlos.

As she turned to face him, Carlos cracked her in the jaw with a second punch. This time, Miko stayed standing. She ate the punch and swallowed that bitch whole, head snapping sideways again but rebounding to face Carlos right away. She stuck out her tongue at him.

"Look at that! You see that? My jaw should have fractured on the first punch, and after two hits like that, I should be preparing to eat through a straw for a few weeks after they wired it back together. But I'm fine! Can you believe it? I'm fine! My body must have responded to the broken finger injury by causing my bones to become denser."

"How can you prove that, though?" Carlos asked her.

Miko thought for several seconds, then snapped her fingers.

"Scale," she said, then walked over to the digital scale against the wall. "If my bones are significantly denser, then I'm going to weigh more. I weighed one-hundred and twenty-five pounds yesterday."

Miko stepped up on the scales. Two seconds later, the digital display read one-hundred and forty pounds.

"You see that, Carlos?!?" she asked, her voice shrill and excited as she pointed at the display.

"Science, girl!" he said and gave her a high five. "Man, this is too friggin crazy," he said, shaking his head. He stopped and looked at Miko. "But please tell me we're done for now."

Miko nodded. "Oh yeah. We're done."

"So, now what?" Carlos asked.

"Oh, now we fuck," Miko said. Stepping forward, she grabbed Carlos by his shirt and kissed him fiercely before pushing him back onto the exam table.

ALMOST EVERYONE SAT IN THE BREAK ROOM, CALLED TOGETHER BY Miko for a briefing. Each one sipped coffee as they chit-chatted and waited for Esther to arrive. Morozov, Bryan, and Carlos sat on one side of the table, while Ariana and Miko sat across from them.

Esther walked in and sat down across from Morozov and, without greeting anyone, bowed her head, eyes half-lidded. Morozov reached across and tapped the table in Esther's line of sight. Esther raised her head.

"How are you doing?" Morozov signed. "Is the rubber mat soundproofing helping at all?"

Esther held up one hand, fingers extended, palm down, and tilted it side to side.

"At first," Esther signed. "But the closer we get to the signal, the worse it is and the less the mats help. I have to be rolled up inside multiple mats to get any relief. And outside my room, it's damn near unbearable, especially now that we're only one day away."

"I'm so sorry," Morozov replied. "I hope we can investigate the signal quickly and then meet up with another ship so you can get away from it."

Esther sighed, then signed, "Thanks."

Miko stood and spoke, signing for Esther to understand.

"Okay, everyone," Miko began, "thanks for gathering together. I've got some important information to share with you all, information that Carlos and I gained through multiple experiments we conducted over the last couple of days."

"What kind of experiments?" Ariana asked.

"Medical," Miko answered.

The eyebrows of Morozov, Bryan, and Ariana all rose up in interest.

"Medical?" Ariana asked, a hint of horror in her voice.

"Yes, medical," Miko said. "The signal is changing us in significant biological ways. I suspect it has altered our genetic information all the way down to our DNA. Two days ago, I accidentally banged my shin hard on something. It caused a hematoma and split the skin. To start with, it didn't hurt as bad as it should have, but within one hour, it healed up completely. I was shocked. It was amazing, and I knew I needed to conduct some tests to verify my hypothesis that our bodies are now capable of healing at an incredible rate."

She glanced around. Eyebrows were raised, but everyone seemed to be waiting for something more substantial.

"So," Miko continued, "I enlisted Carlos to help me investigate my theory. We took turns performing various incisions on one another. Every one of the wounds healed up in a timely fashion. Every one of them, including a severed femoral artery, stopped bleeding on their own. Muscle, tendons, ligaments, arteries, veins, and fascia knit themselves back together as we watched. And the more we did it, the faster our bodies started to heal."

"Goddamn, Miko," Bryan said. "That had to hurt worse than fire ants crawling in your panties."

"Actually," Carlos cut in, "it didn't hurt much. Some, but not as bad as it would have been before the signal. Not by a long shot."

"Umph," Bryan grunted. "To be honest, the idea of watching you two play pattycake with a scalpel is a bit unnerving." Bryan shook his head and leaned back, crossing his arms.

"Well, hold on then, because it gets worse," Miko said. She laughed lightly but she laughed alone. "I let Carlos smash the tip of my pinky finger with a hammer. The bone even splintered, but it only took about twenty minutes to totally heal up. But the most fascinating part was how our bodies responded to these injuries. Carlos's body adapted to the repetitive injuries by healing faster and faster. So, based on those observations, I suspected that my body might adapt to the bone injury by increasing my overall bone density. To test my theory, I first let Carlos hit me in the jaw as hard as he could ... and I took it, twice. The first one knocked me on my ass, but I got right back up, and the second one didn't even knock me down. So, within a matter of an hour, my body adapted to the finger injury by increasing my bone density *all over*. Not just my finger, but my *entire* skeletal system. And, it would seem, after the first punch, it adapted further within seconds by making my bones grow even more dense. Now, that's more experiential proof verses something you can quantify and document. So, to prove my bones were denser, I weighed myself on the scales. I'm fifteen pounds heavier now than I was two days ago."

"That's crazy, Miko," Ariana said.

"And it gets crazier ..." Miko said, then paused and looked around the table. Everyone but Carlos cast questioning looks at her, mixed with a degree of shock at the level of injuries she and Carlos had inflicted on one another.

"And ..." she said, glancing over at Carlos, "Carlos *regenerated* three fingertips ... at the *same* time."

Mouths gaped; consternation etched across their contorted faces.

"I mean *fully severed*," Miko went on, "and in twelve minutes, he *totally regenerated* all of them."

Carlos raised his hand and wiggled his fingers.

"These three right here," he said, indicating the three fingertips by touching them in succession with his other index finger. "Brand spanking new."

Morozov looked at Miko.

"You cut off Carlos's fingertips?"

"Yes, ma'am," Miko said. "With a laser scalpel."

Morozov's eyes grew big. She blinked, then closed her eyes and placed the fingertips of one hand to her forehead, shaking her head in short, slow movements. After a few seconds, she breathed in deep and blew it out.

"I can see you all think what I did was extreme," Miko said, "but the knowledge we acquired is immensely important. Just understand, I'm summarizing here. I did several tests, progressively increasing the size and depths of the cuts, before I moved onto bigger, more invasive, or destructive tests. I had good reason to believe that we would heal up from the more severe injuries after everything I had already documented."

Bryan looked at Carlos and bumped him with an elbow.

"And your crazy ass agreed to all this shit, huh?" Bryan asked.

"Uh, yeah, man," Carlos said, glancing over at Miko. Miko's wide eyes pleaded with Carlos to not tell them the whole truth, her head shaking back and forth twice in tiny almost imperceptible movements. "Yeah," Carlos continued, "I wanted to know if I have super healing powers now. I couldn't pass that up."

"Goddamn, son," Bryan said, "You ain't got but one oar in the water."

Carlos's face scrunched up, one eye squinting as he looked at Bryan.

"What the hell does that country-ass bullshit even mean, man?" Carlos asked, clearly annoyed.

"It means the wheels are turning but the hamsters have died," Bryan said, pointing both his index fingers at the sides of his skull and circling them like turning wheels. Bryan laughed, but Carlos still looked confused and angry.

"Son of a bitch," Bryan said, "the signal sure hasn't sharpened the knives in your drawer, has it? I'm saying you're fucking crazy, man. I think you're crazy for agreeing to that shit. But ..." Bryan paused and spread his hands wide, palms facing forward. "Each to his own ... and, I might add, I'll give it to ya ... way to take one for the team." Bryan winked at Carlos. "We appreciate your sacrifice, even if we think it's a bit crazy."

Carlos's face fluttered like a butterfly between anger and appreciation for the recognition, unsure which emotion to settle on.

"Okay," Morozov cut back in, "whether we think Miko and Carlos's actions were a bit excessive or brave, in the name of scientific exploration, Miko *is* correct. The information is *invaluable.* Learning what physical changes the signal has caused in our bodies that are beneficial to us will help us articulate later how important this discovery is to mankind."

"Thank you, Captain," Miko said. "But ... there's something else. Something a bit strange."

"For fuck's sake," Bryan said, "all of this so far hasn't been strange? Goddamn, we better brace ourselves for a real doozy now!"

Miko glared at Bryan for a moment but said nothing.

Morozov kicked Bryan's foot under the table and looked at Miko. "Go ahead. Tell us."

"Well," Miko began, "I'm going to have to give you some personal information I'd rather not, but you need to hear it to understand what I'm talking about. Are y'all okay with that?"

"Hell yeah, girl," said Bryan. "Give us the juicy gossip, why dontcha."

Morozov backhanded Bryan's upper arm and cut her eyes at him.

"Continue," Morozov said.

"Well," Miko began, "as you may have guessed, Carlos and I have been having sex the last few days. Well, I ... I wished I didn't have a bad gag reflex, and it wasn't even really a focused thought process, just a frustration I didn't want to deal with. Well, two hours later, it was improved. So, I experimented and told my body to eliminate any gag reflex. Not long afterward, it was gone. So then I decided to try something else, something physically visible. I told my body to increase the size of my breasts." Miko cupped both her breasts with thumb and forefinger underneath. "By the end of the day, I increased a cup size. I don't fit my bras now."

"I knew your tits looked bigger!" Bryan exclaimed, slapping the tabletop.

Morozov slapped his arm again, this time harder.

"What the hell were you doing looking at her tits?" Morozov asked.

Bryan shrugged. "I'm a perceptive guy," he said. "Kinda hard not to notice a change like that when you're around someone all the time. Especially in confined spaces."

Ariana chuckled. "He's right," she said. "I noticed too."

"She saved your ass," Morozov said under her breath to Bryan.

Carlos raised his hand. "I tried it out after Miko told me what she did," he said.

"Oh, hold on," Bryan said, putting both index fingers to his temples and closing his eyes. "Let me guess, I'm betting you wished for … a bigger cock." Bryan dropped his hands and opened his eyes, trying to keep a straight face.

Carlos was looking straight at him, unashamed. "Duh!" he said. "Damn right, I did! And it worked."

Carlos beamed with pride.

"Really?" Ariana asked, and Miko cut her a look she didn't see.

"Oh yeah," Carlos answered, "along with bigger pecs and biceps too." He stood and took off his shirt. "See?" He flexed, and it was obvious his build had changed in size.

"I also tried changing something else physically about myself," Miko confessed, "and it worked as well. I made my tongue longer." She stuck out her tongue, revealing the increased length.

Esther stared at Miko and Carlos, then signed, "Are y'all obsessed with sex right now? You two are fucking," Esther said indicating Carlos and Miko, "and so are you two," she added, indicating Morozov and Bryan. "Ariana is the only one that *doesn't* seem overly interested in sex. Do you think the signal is activating or changing something within your hormonal systems?"

"Actually," Miko said, "I think the elevated sex drive is just a biproduct of an optimized, healthier body overall. So, it just heightens what's already there."

Bryan sat silent, leaning back in his seat, hands folded on his abdomen and eyes closed. After several seconds, Morozov asked him, "What the hell are you doing?"

Bryan opened his eyes and glanced at her. "I'm focusing on making my dick bigger," he said, loudly. "What else would I be doing?

Everyone chuckled except Morozov, who just leaned back and stared at the ceiling.

Esther leaned forward in her chair and sat up straight.

"What the fuck is wrong with y'all?" she signed. "Y'all think all this is a joke? You think the radical transformation of your bodies down to a genetic level is just cool shit? And no one but Ariana seems able to control their sexual desires. Are y'all in fucking high school? Jesus! We don't know what this signal is, who's transmitting it, or what the end goal design is, if any. What if it continues to transform you into something you *do not* want to be? Have y'all thought about that? No. I don't think any of you have. But the longer we're in range of the signal, the longer it will work on you, and none of you have a fucking clue what that will look like in the end."

Esther paused and glared around the table at each of them.

"And yet, here we are," Esther continued, "still headed for the signal instead of abandoning this crazy mission that was *never* our mission to begin with. We should be getting as far away from that signal as we can, as quickly as we can." Esther shook her head in frustration. "I swear to God," she signed, "I think this signal has compromised everyone's judgement. But what the fuck do I know? I'm not in the circle right now because I'm not being affected by the signal. Y'all haven't given a flying fuck about how badly the signal is affecting me. From the beginning, y'all couldn't grow one fuck to give amongst the lot of you, except for Bryan helping me install the rubber matting. Other than that, y'all couldn't be bothered. So, fuck the signal and fuck y'all."

Esther stood up and stormed out, not looking at anyone. Morozov watched her go, mouth hanging open. No one had ever seen Esther lose it like that.

A HUSHED SILENCE FELL ACROSS THE ROOM ONCE ESTHER DEPARTED, and they all exchanged glances of disbelief at what they had just witnessed. Quiet, mild mannered, meek Esther had just lost her shit completely. An unprecedented event in their time with her.

After several seconds, Ariana spoke up. "Okay, folks. We've got to do something for her. We can't just ignore this any longer."

Nods all around the table indicated unanimous agreement.

"I have an idea," Ariana continued. She turned her head to look at Miko. "Miko, can you 3D print the necessary components to perform a cochlear implant surgery on Esther?"

Morozov and Miko both looked surprised.

"You do remember Esther is a deaf culture advocate, right?" Morozov asked. "She's embraced her inability to hear and doesn't look at it as a disability."

"Yeah," Miko said, "and people like her reject any and all attempts to 'fix' them. So, how do you propose we convince her to agree to the procedure?"

Ariana pressed her lips together. "I don't," she told them and looked around the table.

"Are you suggesting we force her to undergo the procedure?" Miko asked.

Ariana hesitated for a second before speaking. "Yes," she said. "I am."

"Hold on," Miko said, raising her hands and drawing the words out in a cautionary tone. "I can't do that … I mean, that would clearly violate the choice we know she has made for her body, and it would violate her trust as well."

Carlos crossed his arms, leaned back in his chair, and stared at Miko across the table.

"Bitch, please!" Carlos said with a head bob and furrowed brow. "Really, Miko?" He cocked his head at her and refused to look away.

Miko swallowed but said nothing. "You gotta be fucking kidding me," Carlos said, more statement than question. "You know what? I'm just going to say this. I don't think you *want* to go there, because *we both know* you are capable of doing just that."

Miko's mouth clapped shut like a trap. Her lips pressed together and curled inward. She looked away from Carlos. The others were scrutinizing her and Carlos's body language, trying to ascertain just what the underlying story was about.

Neither Miko nor Carlos really wanted their shipmates to discover what transpired between them.

"I'll do it," Miko said. "Give me a couple of hours to print the implant and prepare medical for surgery. Also, I'll need to prep an injection to knock her out for the duration of the procedure."

Miko looked around the table, first at Ariana, then Bryan and Morozov, and lastly, Carlos.

"Just to be clear, though," she said, "I'm doing the surgical procedure ... but all of you are responsible for getting her to the table. That's my only stipulation."

Morozov nodded. "Very well," she agreed. "I hate that we have to do this to her, but I know it's for her own good. We don't even know if the signal is actually damaging her body. The way she looks and feels, it's certainly possible, though. I have to agree with Ariana. We need to do this for Esther." Morozov turned to Miko. "Miko, please let us know when you have the implant parts produced and you're ready to get started. We'll grab Esther at that time."

"Will do," Miko replied. "I'm going to head to Medical and get started." She stood and walked out, dreading what was to come. Hurting Carlos was one thing. She was sure he would heal. But this, this was a blatant attack on who Esther was at her core. A violation of her very identity. Miko tried to tell herself maybe Morozov was right. Maybe the signal was hurting her or changing her in very negative ways. If it were true, then the implant procedure would definitely be in Esther's best health interests.

It's not like she can't have it removed later if she chooses, Miko thought.

ESTHER HURRIED BACK TO HER ROOM. ONCE INSIDE, SHE RETRIEVED her tablet and tapped into the ship's internal surveillance system. All of the communal areas had multiple motion activated micro video cameras mounted around the rooms to catch nearly every angle. It was just a matter of accessing the recordings. And Esther knew how. Morozov had her do it once before, and she was betting the captain had not changed her access code since then.

Esther opened a window, accessed the ship's systems, and traced a connection to ship security, then entered Morozov's code and selected Surveillance Recordings.

She accessed the most recent recordings of the break room. Once opened, she swiped slowly to her left until she spotted herself walking out and stopped it there. She did the same thing with the other recordings, then hit play on one. It was tedious work, much like putting a puzzle together, but she played one video at a time, attempting to follow the conversation in the order it occurred. Some parts were not discernable, but she understood enough to grasp the gist of their conversation. It horrified her. She didn't want to believe it was true. She double-checked her findings, hoping she interpreted things wrong, but it wasn't so.

When she had confirmed what her crewmates were planning, it was a brutal punch to the gut. She set the tablet down and stood up, mind racing. Adrenaline coursed through her body, making her feel the need to pace around the room, but her head spun, and she leaned against the wall. A pang of terror twisted in her gut like a knife and creeped up into her throat. The thought of being fully exposed to the signal horrified her and made her nauseous. There was no way she could allow them to put a cochlear implant in her head.

Esther struggled to calm her mind and decide on an optimal course of action to thwart their plans.

There really aren't many options, she finally concluded with a sigh. *Can't barricade or block a sliding door with what I have available to me.*

I've got to lock myself in here, which means short circuiting the door's locking system, she thought. *But how?*

She snapped her fingers and picked her tablet back up. Esther clicked through the various communal cameras, hoping to locate her crewmates, or at least determine where they likely were. Ariana sat on the bridge at her station, reading. Miko was in medical preparing for the surgery. But the others were nowhere to be seen.

Must be in their quarters, she hoped, then attempted to hurry out the door. It was more like a hasty stagger, one hand bracing on the corridor wall to keep her upright. She held the tablet in one hand and looked at it every few seconds to monitor the cameras as she headed for the engine room. The short trip there was without incident, and no one appeared to be moving about on the camera feeds.

She entered the room and began scanning. It took her a minute to spot it, but Esther finally found what she was looking for—the variable-powered battery pack. After checking to make sure all the wires and cables were inside the black mesh bag next to it, she picked up both the battery pack and the bag and stacked them on a collapsible dolly. As she turned to exit the room, she stopped suddenly, looked around, grabbed a large flathead screwdriver with a thick rubberized handle, then picked up a hammer as well. She put them in the mesh bag and made her way back to her room.

Esther pried a panel off the wall outside her room with the screwdriver. Underneath it was the electronics that controlled the door from the hallway side. She took the screwdriver and placed it on an area containing numerous circuits, then hammered it through the electronics into the wall. She hooked up both wires to the metal portion of the screwdriver, stretched them out, and pulled them inside the room with her, then she turned the battery pack on and selected the max power setting. She closed the door to her room, holding up the wires so they didn't get pulled off the screwdriver by accident.

Here goes nothing, she thought, and picked up the ends of the wires.

One at a time, she plugged in the wires to the battery pack. When the second one slid in and made contact, Esther heard the crackle of electricity pop, sizzle, and spit as she watched sparks fly across the hallway through the camera feed outside her room.

"Yes," Esther said and raised both her hands in victory. She double-checked her work and tried to open the door. It didn't move.

I'm locked in here now, she thought. *No turning back.* It all felt so surreal. Just a few days ago, she never could have foreseen these developments, her life reaching this place. She talked herself through the plan.

Okay. Now, I'll leave the battery pack hooked up. Whoever touches it first will get a good jolt.

She wondered if it might hurt one of them badly, or kill them, but after what she saw Miko say her and Carlos had healed up from, Esther didn't think death was a concern. She walked over to the bunk beds, pulled out the carbon fiber hair stick she used to keep her hair up, and laid it on the bedside table. She laid down on the rubber matting, pulled it over her in a dome shape, and watched the tablet screen, waiting for the camera feed to reveal her shipmates coming to take her away. To trample her wishes and identity by violating her body.

It didn't take long before she fell asleep.

MOROZOV AND BRYAN WALKED SIDE BY SIDE WITH CARLOS AND Ariana following behind them. Morozov carried the autoinjector with the sedative Miko had prepared. As they approached Esther's door, Bryan spoke out.

"Oh, for fuck's sake," he said. "This goat ropin' is about to graduate into a full-on rodeo."

"What the fuck are you talking about, farm boy?" Carlos asked, frustrated once more with Bryan's unfathomable slang. "Do you even speak modern English, motherfucker?"

Bryan ignored Carlos's questions.

"Look at this," Bryan said, holding out one hand to indicate the damaged panel and the wires leading from the screwdriver embedded in the wall to inside the room. "She's fried the door controls and locked herself in her room."

"Well," Carlos asked Bryan, "do you think you can bypass this mess and open the door?"

"Maybe," Bryan said, shrugging. "Depends on how bad it's damaged." Bryan lifted his ball cap up and down, scratching his forehead with it as he assessed the door and contemplated how they got into this situation. "How the hell do you reckon she found out what we had planned?" Bryan asked the others.

Carlos shrugged. Ariana stood there looking like his shadow, her shoulders rising and falling as well.

"I think I know how," Morozov said. "A while back, I had Esther help me with something and I gave her access to the communal area surveillance cams, as well as my security code, and let her run with it. Sneaky little bitch must have memorized my code. I'm betting when she left, she logged in and accessed the feeds from where she walked out until we left. There are multiple feed angles. I'm sure she was able to read all our lips."

"Smart girl," said Ariana,

"Sneaky little bitch," Morozov said with a half-smile. "That's what she is. I didn't realize she had it in her." Morozov grinned widely, a little proud of Esther.

"Okay," Bryan cut in. "Y'all wait here while I run to the engine room and get some tools. I'll be right back."

Bryan started to walk away but stopped and looked back. "And *don't touch* anything," he said, eying Carlos, then turned and left.

As soon as he was out of sight, Carlos stepped up to look at the panel. He bent forward, staring at the damaged area. After several seconds of inspection, Carlos determined the proper course of action.

"This ain't that difficult. All we have to do is pull out the screwdriver and conduct a function check."

Carlos reached out toward the screwdriver slowly.

"I wouldn't do that," Ariana warned. "Bryan said not to touch anything."

"Bryan's not the only one who can fix something around here," Carlos said, ignoring her as he continued extending his hand slowly until he gripped the thick rubber handle.

Nothing happened.

"See," he said to Ariana. "It's fine."

Carlos tugged on the screwdriver handle. It didn't budge. He yanked harder and harder, then threw his whole body backwards in an attempt to dislodge the tool. Still, it didn't budge.

"Dammit!" he complained. "Is this fucking thing named Excalibur or something? It's stuck in there good."

He leaned in, gripping the handle tightly, and reached out to place his left hand beside the removed panel to brace himself as he attempted once more to pull the screwdriver from the door controls.

There was a loud pop and sizzle, accompanied by a flash of blue-white light filling the hallway the exact moment Carlos touched the wall. Morozov and Ariana shielded their eyes and turned away from the blinding luminescence. They heard, but did not see, Carlos's limp body strike the opposite wall, then hit the floor.

"UUMMPH!"

The impact knocked the wind out of Carlos's lungs as his back hit the wall first, followed by his head bouncing off the metal surface. His whole body felt on fire for a moment, and then it began dwindling in intensity to a steady hum and painful tingle. His ears rang. He couldn't breathe. Shaking his head, Carlos pushed up to his hands and knees and struggled to take a breath. The world spun, a black, starless vortex spinning about him as it sucked at his consciousness. He felt a touch on his shoulder and focused on it.

Within a few seconds, he managed to open his eyes and breathe in. He swayed like a small boat on rough seas, but he was awake and slowly recovering.

"That bitch ... electrocuted me ... didn't she?" Carlos asked the others in between breaths.

"Yeah," replied Morozov. "Pretty much."

"Fuck," Carlos said, breathing hard as he stood up and leaned against the wall.

Morozov and Ariana stood on each side of him, both women gripping a wrist with one hand while hooking under his bicep with their free arm to support him.

"I don't think ... " Carlos began, "I would have lived through that ... before the signal ... bitch would've killed me."

"Don't tell me," Bryan called out from down the hall as he approached, "he fucking touched the panel, didn't he?"

Morozov looked his way and nodded.

"For fuck's sake," Bryan said aloud. "If that boy's brains were dynamite, he couldn't even blow his nose."

"Fuck you, man," Carlos said, hands on his knees, bent over.

"Seriously, man," Bryan continued, "did you not see the wires leading from the screwdriver to inside the room? What the hell do you suppose those wires are attached to?"

Bryan paused as he came to a stop.

"Well?" Bryan taunted Carlos, but he didn't bite. He just looked away and shut his mouth.

"I'd bet my next paycheck," Bryan said, "that those wires are hooked to a battery pack. The variable power battery pack that's missing from the engine room, specifically. She used it to short out the control panel and lock herself in, then left it hooked up. The whole door and wall are booby-trapped."

"I told him it wasn't a good idea," Ariana said. "I had a feeling it might be rigged."

Carlos groaned. "Spare me the 'I told you so' routine, you two," he said.

"Well," Ariana replied, "you were this close to becoming a

Darwin Award winner." She held up one hand, thumb and index finger no more than a couple of centimeters apart. "Maybe you should take our advice to heart before something kills you."

Carlos got ready to say something, but Morozov cut her eyes at him.

"Don't," Morozov said. "Just don't."

Morozov turned her attention to Bryan.

"Okay, Bryan," she said. "Can you get us in there?"

"For you, sweet tits," he answered, grinning wide, "absolutely."

Ariana's jaw dropped, and Morozov's eyes narrowed to slits as she glared at him. Bryan's lips pursed and twisted to one side as his eyebrows arched upward.

"Captain Sweet Tits?" Bryan asked, his tone playful but skiddish. Morozov wasn't smiling. In fact, she looked like the proverbial bear, and Bryan had just poked it. Twice.

"Bryan," Morozov said through gritted teeth. "We are not in my quarters on our own time. We are among crewmates. Call me anything other than Captain, ma'am, or sir out here again, and I will punch you right in your goddamn mouth. Understood?"

Bryan's lips curled inward again as she spoke, and he resisted the temptation to cover his mouth with a hand. Struggling to return his mouth to a neutral position and adopt a straight face, he flattened his lips and clenched his teeth together. On one hand, he wanted to laugh for getting her riled up. On the other hand, he didn't want nothing to do with her if she really flew hot.

"Yes, ma'am," Bryan said. "Clear as crystal."

"Good," Morozov said, then breathed in and blew the air out sharply through her nose. "Now, back to business. Open the damn door without getting the shit shocked out of you."

"Aye, aye, Captain," Bryan replied, then set down the tool kit he was carrying. He dug into it and pulled out a pair of completely rubberized pliers. The ends were coated in thick, texturized rubber to enhance grip and eliminate any chance of conductivity. Bryan gripped one of the wires where it connected to the screwdriver, then grabbed the handle of the screwdriver, being sure to not allow any part of his body to touch the wall. He pulled on the wires while he pushed on the screwdriver handle, and the first wire came loose. He gripped the second wire with the pliers and repeated his efforts. Both wires were now detached. He kept the ends separated and set them on the floor.

"Okay," Bryan informed them, "the boobytrap is disarmed. Now to see how jacked up the controls are."

He inspected the circuits surrounding the embedded screwdriver, identifying the different relays and noting whether they were a fused mess or still somewhat intact. When he finished, Bryan took a second pass, scrutinizing everything once more before delivering a prognosis.

"This thing's deader than a bag of hammers," Bryan declared.

"How are we going to get in then?" Ariana asked.

"I've got a manual rig for opening these doors in case of emergencies," Bryan informed her. "See these two slots in the door right here?" Bryan asked as he pointed at the location on the door.

"Yeah," Ariana said, nodding.

"The rig has a piece that slides into those slots, and then you basically have to work a lever back and forth like an old mechanical jack and it'll pry the door open. Standby and I'll go get it ... and nobody touch anything while I'm gone. Capiche?"

Bryan didn't wait for an answer from anyone, not even Carlos. He just turned and walked away.

ESTHER WATCHED HER SHIPMATES APPROACH THE DOOR, THEN STAND around discussing what to do. She made out phrases and words here and there, depending on who was facing more towards the camera when they spoke. After some discussion, Bryan left.

Dammit, she thought. *He's going to get some tools and come back and bypass what I did.*

She began considering what her Plan B would be when she had nowhere to go. Options were slim.

And then she saw Carlos reach out and grab the screwdriver handle.

Oh, you dumb motherfucker, she thought. *C'mon. Touch the wall, or the door, or the panel. Anywhere around there will do.*

She saw Carlos's other hand extend towards the wall. It was immediately followed by a large flash of light on the screen and Carlos flying across the hall to strike the opposing wall, then hit the floor.

"Holy shit!" she exclaimed aloud just before a hand flew up to cover her mouth. She leaned closer to the screen, staring at Carlos, praying he wasn't dead. That wasn't her intention.

She was glad when Carlos began to move around and eventually stood up. She had not realized the battery could deliver such a powerful charge. Esther watched them but paid close attention to Bryan when he returned and began assessing the door controls. In the end, she felt relieved when Bryan told them the door controls were dead.

The feeling didn't last long, though. She couldn't make it out entirely, but she suspected Bryan left to retrieve some type of tool or tools to get through the door. The waiting was the worst. Her thoughts sprinted like rabbits flushed from their holes, danger at every turn–right, left, behind, and above, always above. What would she do? What could a little rabbit do against a pack of foxes? Or a flock of hungry hawks circling and darting in after their prey? She had no control. They would drug her, take her, fix her, then make her hear the signal ... and ... be just like them. They would control her body, her choices. They would make her vulnerable to the signal's influence, to the changes it would make to her body and mind as it was doing to them.

She needed a means of control. Some small mechanism by which she could affect change, even from her current position of weakness.

Bryan's return to the video feed caught her eye and hooked her attention once more. He had wheeled a large metal contraption in front of the door, and whatever it was, she didn't think she'd ever seen one before, much less had any idea what it did.

BRYAN UNLOADED THE DOOR JACK.

"What took you so long?" Morozov asked.

"I sprayed all the contact points of this thing down with a quick-dry rubberized coating," Bryan replied. "Just in case Esther gets creative while we're working here."

Morozov nodded. "Good thinking."

With Carlos's help, the two men positioned the jack in between the door jambs, halfway up the door in line with two identical slots cut side by side into the door itself. It was clear they were part of the original door design.

Bryan used one hand to adjust two thick metal prongs until they slipped into the slots on the door. Once they were in place, he and Carlos held it steady.

"Captain, can you grab the wheel and turn it clockwise until I tell you to stop, please?" Bryan asked.

"Sure," she said, and stepped forward. She turned the wheel quickly, and the ends extended outward until each one pressed into a side of the door jamb and wedged the mechanism in place.

"That's good," Bryan told Morozov, then released the jack and stepped back, eying it to verify it was level. Carlos and Morozov stepped back as well. Bryan retrieved a long bar. One end of it appeared freshly coated with rubber. He slipped the metal end into a round housing that moved and began levering the bar from right to left. As he moved the bar fully to the right and then fully to the left, the metal object with the prongs wedged into the door moved slowly from the right to the left, gradually opening the door.

After moving the lever side to side a few times, Bryan saw a crack of light where the door now separated from the wall.

ESTHER SAT FROZEN WITH FEAR, WATCHING BRYAN OPERATE THE JACK. She shifted her eyes from the entrance to the tablet multiple times. But she couldn't see if the door was actually moving. Scrambling over to the door, she placed her hand on it. She felt it moving and knew it was just a matter of seconds before Bryan made enough space for them to enter. Her brain floundered for any possible option she might have.

And then it came to her, just as the door opened a crack. If she was able to shock them before, then she could do it again. She scrabbled for the wires, gripped them, and snatched them into the room. She carefully grabbed an end in each hand, touched them together to verify they were still hot, then touched them to the door as she watched the tablet.

Nothing.

There was no big flash of light. No image of Bryan being thrown across the hallway.

Why the fuck isn't this working? her brain shrieked in a panic. She repeated the process, touching the door in two different locations.

Still nothing.

She looked at the door. There was a good six inch opening now. Big enough for an arm. Soon it would be large enough for Morozov to slip through. Esther dropped the wires, not knowing Bryan had thwarted her plan before she even conceived it. She retreated to her bed, eying the door with dread and distrust.

She had to do something now. In another minute, they would rush in here and fall upon her. Then there would be no opportunity left for her to take control of her life. Her body. Esther looked around, scanning the room for anything she could use. And that was when her eyes fell upon a specific object.

The carbon fiber hair stick.

BRYAN HAD MANAGED TO JACK THE DOOR OPEN BETWEEN TWENTY-FIVE to thirty centimeters when Morozov knelt beneath him and tried to look through the opening without touching the door or surrounding wall. She leaned close to the door jamb and peeked inside the room. She saw Esther sitting on the top bunk of the bed and made eye contact with her. The determination on Esther's face was mixed with hurt and betrayal. It asked Morozov, *Why have you pushed me this far?*

That was when Morozov saw what Esther was holding to the side of her head. The girl was gripping a hair stick tightly in one hand with the exposed pointy end sticking in her ear. She reached over the top of her head, closed her eyes, and slammed her palm against the bottom of her fist.

Morozov screamed, "Esther, no!" as a good eight centimeters of the hair stick drove into Esther's ear, piercing the eardrum and tympanic nerve clusters. Esther wailed and tilted sideways, but she was resolute.

"Hurry up!" Morozov hollered at Bryan. "Hurry the fuck up!"

Esther switched hands, placed the hair stick in her other ear, and began reaching over her head the opposite direction this time.

"Please, Esther," Morozov signed, hoping the girl would look and see. "Don't hurt yourself like this. You don't have to do this. Please."

Morozov moved to squeeze through the opening now, but as she turned sideways and slipped through, she heard Esther's voice pronouncing judgement on her as the captain.

"You pushed me to this," Esther said aloud. "You allowed it."

As Morozov squeezed through the other side, Esther slammed her palm down on her fist and drove the hair stick through her opposite ear, then she laid on her side and shrieked in pain, tears flowing down her cheeks. She dropped the bloody hair stick on her white sheets, and they turned red beneath it.

Morozov wanted to comfort Esther, but the girl flinched away from her touch.

Morozov moved back toward the door. Shaking her head, she turned and called to Bryan.

"Tell Miko to bring her medkit and meet us here ASAP!"

"I'VE GOT HER SEDATED, FOR NOW," MIKO INFORMED MOROZOV. "I managed to laser suture the holes in her eardrums but I'm unsure just how extensive the damage to the nerve clusters is and whether that will cause her ongoing pain or not. We'll just have to wait and see, but for now, at least, she's asleep."

Morozov stared down at the sleeping Esther, the pain of failing the young girl clearly etched into her face.

"How did I let it come to this?" she asked out loud. She didn't expect an answer from Miko. She continued speaking and answered her own question. "By ignoring her pain and suffering," Morozov confessed, her tone both remorseful and disgusted with herself. "That's how … Goddammit …"

Morozov was quiet, and the moment seemed to drag out and dangle in the gulf between her and Miko until it seemed it might strangle itself and perish, trapping them in that room, staring at her failure as a captain, unable to look away.

At last, Morozov managed to compose her thoughts and spoke, breaking the spell.

"Keep me informed of her condition, please," she said and turned to walk away.

"Yes, ma'am," Miko responded, watching Morozov exit her office, Esther's pain weighing on her like the Earth on the shoulders of Atlas.

6

ESTHER WOKE, THIS TIME MORE FULLY THAN ANY OF THE THREE TIMES before when she had drifted up onto the shores of consciousness and been immediately swept back into an ocean of blissful rest. She cracked her eyelids and tried to look around for Miko or anyone else without revealing she was awake.

She spotted Miko sitting at her desk and facing one of the side monitors, her back to Esther. Esther turned her head enough to cut her eyes upward and see the IV Med system pumping meds into her veins on a timetable. She slowly reached over and grabbed the tubing, crimped it, and stuffed it under her upper thigh and buttocks. Her other hand was strapped to the table. She tested it. It wasn't super tight, but it was snug. She didn't dare raise her head too high, but she suspected it was some form of ratchet strap Bryan probably dug up from the cargo bay.

Esther still felt groggy, but that would change in the next couple of hours as the drugs worked their way out of her system and were not replaced. Then her mind would be clear, and she'd be able to physically function well enough to attempt escape.

She closed her eyes and fell back asleep, dreaming of how she would break free.

FIVE DAYS TRAVELLED - ARRIVAL AT THE SIGNAL'S SOURCE

CARLOS TURNED OFF THE AUTOPILOT AND GRIPPED THE CONTROLS before they exited Faster than Light travel to arrive at their destination. They knew at once they were in the right location, no doubt about it. A deep, powerful bass hummed and thrummed, strumming the cords of their flesh and tickling their brains. The increased strength of the signal was instantly palpable the moment they dropped out of FTL.

Morozov sat in her captain chair behind Carlos, elevated above his position. Ariana and Miko stood next to her, one on each side, while Bryan stood behind her.

An audible gasp escaped from them in unison, both from the feelings that struck their bodies and the sight outside the bridge window.

The signal's source.

Before them loomed what appeared to be a massive tear in space, in the very fabric of the universe. It was a vertical wound ripping through the empty blackness and peeling it back along warped and puckered edges to reveal a red and purple cosmic tissue of sorts beneath the darkness. Stretching between the edges of the opening were densely knit ropey threads of both thick and thin construction, connecting one side to the other in a crisscrossing series of spiderweb-like structures. They looked as if they were stretched taut, as if an unknown form or force on the other side was slowly pushing its way through or, at the least, positioning itself on the border of their universe. Either way, it seemed to be spreading the interwoven dermal layers of their dimension further and further apart.

They all looked on in wonder and curiosity. The sounds and feel of the signal were like a lover now, the unique combination of harmonic frequencies bathing both body and mind in their beauty. But staring into the rift, they each had to wonder just what *was* on the other side, and was it trying to come through?

"Ariana," Morozov said, "please run analysis on the rift as well as the signal again now that we're here. Carlos, move us in a little closer ... but not too close."

"Aye, aye, Captain," Carlos said and activated two of the rear thrusters to maneuver them forward gently.

Ariana nodded, then moved to sit at her workstation, where she began running scans and analysis algorithms on both the rift and the signal.

"Geez!" Bryan remarked. "That thing looks like a big ass spider spun a funnel web in a huge cosmic vagina ... and ... and it's that time of the month." Bryan's cheeks rose and nostrils sneered in disgust, forcing his eyes to squint.

"For fuck's sake, Bryan," Morozov complained, face twisting, clearly repulsed by his commentary.

Bryan shrugged. "I just call 'em like I see 'em, boss," he said.

"Captain?" Ariana called out.

"Go."

"The signal strength has increased by fivefold from what it was just prior to our arrival. Content and make up is the same except for two additions. It's like there's two overlapping choruses in the background now. One is higher pitched, an almost angelic combination of voices, while the other is low with alternating vibrations, and perhaps instruments as well. It almost sounds like a mixture of throat singing, a deep horn, and maybe a Celtic chant. I'm not entirely sure. It's hard to pin it down enough to identify without further study ... but ... I don't know about y'all, but I'm feeling fucking fantastic right now. I mean, even better than before. I'm at ease too. Like I know everything's gonna be all right."

Ariana paused, and Bryan suddenly cut in, his voice deep and full as he sang a song he remembered from the days of his youth when he attended church during summer bible camp. Bryan's voice boomed and reverberated within the limited space of the bridge, but his eyes were focused on the rift in space before them.

"Oh, Oh, I … I got a feeling … everything's gonna be all right … Woah, woah, I … I got a feeling … everything's gonna be all right … Oh, Oh, I … I got a feeling … everything's gonna be all right, gonna be all right, gonna be all right, gonna be all right …"

Morozov stared at Bryan in disbelief.

"Miko," Ariana said, "draw blood from each of us and run a chemical panel. Specifically, dopamine, serotonin, and endorphins, along with anything else that might directly influence how we feel."

"On it," Miko said. She reached in her bag and produced five hypodermic blood test kits.

Ariana closed her eyes and cocked her head to one side, conducting a self-assessment. After several seconds, she added, "And look for anything that will make us more trusting or attached in general. I'm definitely feeling a greater sense of belonging in the presence of the signal's source, but I also feel that same sensation and emotional attachment toward the rift there, as if I'm meant to go there. My mind is being swayed somehow. No doubt about it."

A short time later, the lab results started rolling in. Miko pulled them up in separate windows at Esther's station and scanned through each person's readout, first noting and comparing dopamine, serotonin, and endorphin levels with prior test results.

"Ariana," Miko announced, "you are correct. We all have markedly higher levels of dopamine, serotonin, and endorphins in our blood currently. Now, give me a minute. I'm going to look through here for any other abnormally high scores."

Her eyes moved rapidly as she scanned down her own test results first. Near the bottom, she identified another outlier, marked it, and continued to the end. Nothing else. She then went through the others' tests one by one, still assessing them as a whole but also specifically seeking to compare her one outlying number to their scores for the same chemical. With each person's results, her eyebrows creeped higher on her forehead.

"Well," Miko said, "this is rather interesting. We all have one other chemical in our blood that is not just unusually high but extraordinarily high. Like, ridiculously high."

"What is it?" Morozov asked.

"Oxytocin," Miko replied, and looked around at the others, assessing their faces to see if they knew what it was and what it implied. A flicker of recognition registered on Ariana's furrowed brow, but she couldn't seem to place it. The others had no clue.

"What the hell is oxytocin?" Bryan asked. "Sounds like one of them old school pain pills that people used to get addicted to."

"No, Bryan," Miko answered. "It has nothing to do with pain relief."

"Then what does it do?" Morozov cut in.

"Well, for women, it's involved in giving birth, milk production, and bonding with their baby, but it's also referred to as the love hormone. Studies have proved that it can actually improve relationships." Miko said. "Oxytocin is a chemical produced by our hypothalamus that helps people bond with one another and improves trust and long-term commitment. Typically, physical acts of affection are responsible for the production of oxytocin. Holding hands, hugging, kissing, sex. Now, knowing how much sex we've been having, I could possibly attribute the high levels partially to that, but correct me if I'm wrong, Ariana ..." Miko turned and looked at her friend, then continued to speak. "But you haven't had sex during the last few days, have you? Or any other significant physical contact with anyone?"

"Nope," Ariana said, shaking her head side to side. "Not at all. I've been reading and studying the whole time. Y'all four are the ones who have been fucking like rabbits." Ariana swept her index finger back and forth across all of them. "Not that I'm judging," she added. "More power to ya. Especially you and the captain, Bryan.

Y'all both needed a good fuck if anybody around here did. I'm happy for you both."

Morozov sputtered but couldn't think of anything to respond with. Bryan looked at Ariana, chuckled, and shook a finger at her.

"I could complain and call foul, but why bother?" Bryan asked. "You are correctamundo, girl! Boy did I *ever* need it and how!"

"Okay," Miko said, "settle down, big man. Let's get back to the results. The sex alone can't account for numbers this high; however, there are two other things which have been shown to increase oxytocin levels. One is exercise, but Ariana also rules that one out with her constant reading, so it leaves just one other source capable of increasing oxytocin production that we have all experienced recently—music. Music can increase it, especially when it's music experienced together or sung together. Which means, it *has* to be the signal. The signal is activating increased production of oxytocin at an unbelievably high level to make us feel closer to it, to each other, and to feel bonded and invested in the signal and, I suspect, its source. It probably increased our levels some when we first started hearing the signal and helped push us into coming here to begin with, and now it's possible the levels are increasing further so we won't want leave until the signal is done working in us ... or ..." Miko paused, "or because the signal wants us to come join it, and the increased oxytocin levels are making us more trusting and willing to commit to the final plunge, so to say."

"You mean go inside that space vagina?" Bryan asked with a straight face—except for one cocked eyebrow.

"Yes, Bryan," Miko said, flustered. "Look, just consider how dramatically our bodies and intellectual capacity for learning have been improved thus far. How much further can the signal take us if we go right to the source? It could be the trigger for the next evolutionary jump in human development at a genetic level. If we can bring back these changes, or at least bring back proof that leads to more people coming here, it could shape the future of mankind. I know on the surface, things may appear a little sketchy, but I think we need to go all the way, take the final leap and see what we become. I think there's enough evidence so far to justify taking the risk. What do y'all think?"

Miko looked around at everyone but then let her eyes meet Morozov's with a questioning gaze.

Ariana, Bryan, and Carlos deferred to Morozov, waiting to see what she would say first.

"I'm not making this decision on my own," Morozov said after several seconds of deep thought, shaking her head. "What say you all?" She glanced around the room, looking each one in the eyes.

"You know I'm in," Miko said.

"Me too," Carlos spoke up. "I never could have dreamed of doing some of the things I can now. I want to see where it all goes."

Bryan lit a cigar, puffed on it twice, then inhaled deeply and blew it out. "I'm in, Captain, if you are," he said.

"What about Esther?" Morozov asked Miko. "What are we going to do with her? We can't fix her hearing now."

"We sedate her," Miko answered bluntly. "Part of her problem is the level of stress it's generating in her body. If she's unconscious, I strongly suspect it will be mitigated to a large degree. Also, we can stick her in the cryo pod in the escape pod. It'll keep her under, and it should keep her healthy until we get back to a real med lab and away from the signal. Besides, who knows, when we reach the signal's source, it may be strong enough to effect change on her body and mind despite her hearing loss. There's no way to tell, though. It's all hypothetical. But I think it's worth the risk."

Morozov nodded.

"Agreed," Morozov said. "Okay then, Miko. You convinced me. I'm game. Let's do this."

ESTHER WOKE TO THE FEELING OF THE BASS COMPONENTS OF THE signal reverberating through the ship and her body. It was horrible.

She felt as if she were a tuning fork being continuously struck over and over again by each repetitious note. Her body quivered. Her brain vibrated in her skull. And neither ceased. There was no relief.

It was hell.

And now that the pain medication was out of her system, both her ears burned and throbbed terribly, and the signal only made it worse. Her head spun and ached, but her mental faculties were not compromised by drugs any longer. However, that also meant she was completely on her own, without any assistance of any kind to help deal with the pain in her ears or with the signal and its physical and mental effects upon her.

She strained to focus her mind on one thing at a time.

Escape? Maybe. Disable ship? Why? It just leaves me here to suffer. Take over ship and set course for nearest mining colony or space station? How? How the fuck could I possibly pull that off? Kill. I could kill them. They won't expect me to be violent. Not little meek Esther. No way. But how? How can I kill them? I can't overpower them. I'm not sure if I can even walk right now, and even with a pipe or knife, I couldn't face more than one at a time, and there's no guarantees of that. I'd need a firearm. But dammit, Morozov is the only one with the access codes to open the armory. Fuck! Fuck, fuck, fuck, fuck! Arrggghh. What can I do? God, what can I do? Reason with them? Hah! No fucking way. Won't happen. Won't do any fucking good. Might as well just lay here and let the meds flow again.

Esther gave up on brainstorming potential solutions. There was only one option for her.

Escape. That's it. That's all I got. Get out of here. Grab my space suit. Get to the escape pod. Launch. Set course and get in the cryo pod. That's my best bet. Okay. That's the plan. Now, step one. Get the fuck out of here.

Esther turned her attention to the IV trying to drug her first. She rolled toward the hand pinned down by the strap until she could reach the medical port mounted to the top of her right forearm where the IV line hooked in. She grabbed the circular metal base with her fingers, twisted it a half-turn counter-clockwise, uncoupled it, and pulled the line out. Once free from the IV, she tried to sit up and look at the strap holding her left arm in place. A stabbing pain shot through her skull from ear to ear, and a wave of nausea rolled through her stomach. She laid back down. She'd seen it, and she was right. It was a cargo ratchet strap. She rolled toward it and pressed the release down with her right hand and lifted her arm up, relieving the tension enough to slip her hand free.

Yes! she thought. *Step one almost complete. Now, get on your fucking feet and get out of this room.*

Easing herself up on one forearm, Esther waited a few seconds, then sat up as she swung her legs over the edge. She sat still and assessed her stability. The pain was at a solid just-give-me-the-fucking-drugs level, but she would have to just deal. The nausea was less now, thankfully, but her equilibrium was trashed. She'd have sworn someone was spinning the bed beneath her.

You'll fucking crawl, Esther ordered herself, then answered, *Yes, ma'am!*

She slid off the bed onto the floor on all fours and crawled over to Miko's medicine cabinet. Once there, she managed to stand, holding on to the counter and doors. She found an auto-injector along with one vial containing four sedative doses and two pain vials with five doses each. She loaded the sedative vial and dialed it up to four doses at once. She scanned over Miko's examination instruments and found one of the larger rubber-coated mallets. She bit into the rubber and tore at it with her teeth until she peeled the rubber off to expose the metal below.

With hammer in left hand and the auto-injector in her right hand, she crawled toward the door.

MIKO DID NOT HURRY AS SHE MOVED THROUGH THE SHIP'S HALLWAYS back to her med lab. She had no reason to believe Esther was anything but fully sedated and strapped to the bed. It would be an easy task to provide a pre-cryostasis sedative and move her down to the escape pod on a mag lev gurney and place her in the cryo pod there.

Her mind was not concerned with Esther. Instead, it was focused on what might lay before them, what it would be like inside the rift. Her thoughts raced as she imagined what they would become when united with the signal's source. Visions were dancing through her head when she reached the med lab and walked through the door.

Esther, on all fours and approaching the door from the side along the wall, was surprised at Miko's entrance but noticed at once the woman had not seen her right away. She did, however, stop immediately a few feet inside the door when she saw that Esther was not on the bed.

Before Miko could turn around, Esther reached out, gripping Miko's left ankle in one hand while she plunged the autoinjector into the woman's calf and held it there. Miko reflexively tried to yank her leg away but couldn't free it in time. The quadruple dose of sedative entered her system and hit her an instant later. She staggered. One leg gave out halfway, but she remained on her feet, swaying in place like a skinny tree in a hurricane but still standing. Miko tried to look down at Esther, but her vision blurred and the world spun.

Esther switched the hammer to her right hand and swung it, striking Miko in the side of her knee. The leg gave out, and Miko fell backwards, rolling onto one side. Esther swung the hammer again, this time striking Miko in the forehead.

She felt a deep THUD, and Miko lay still, a large hematoma swelling up from the skin centered between and just above her eyebrows. Esther paused and looked at the woman's eyes.

Consciousness. Woozy, swirling consciousness, but consciousness nonetheless. Miko still wasn't out completely. Esther cringed inside. She didn't want to follow through with this, but her fear of the signal was greater than her distaste for committing violence. She swung the hammer again, this time hitting the top edge of the prior wound. Another THUD and an overlapping hematoma began to rise. Again. THUD. Shockwaves ran up through her arm from the intensity of the impact. This time the hematomas erupted with blood where the two met, bursting across Miko's face and into her hairline while splattering up into Esther's eyes, red dots sprinkling over her skin.

Miko's eyes were still open but rolling about as if searching for something unseen. Again, Esther swung the hammer down, hard as she could and dropping her shoulder into it. She felt the woman's skull give, felt something break, perhaps. Miko's eyes closed, and her body went limp at last. Dead or unconscious, Esther wasn't sure, but she wasn't waiting around to check.

Using her shirt, she wiped her eyes and face, then began crawling toward the door, fighting nausea and pain. Once outside, she hurried as quickly as she could manage without losing balance. Each time she picked a hand up or slid a knee forward, her body wobbled side to side but never fell over.

First stop was the space suit locker by the airlock. She'd suit up, then head to the escape pod.

Bryan left the bridge and headed toward the engine room to shut down the primary engine for entry into the rift. He'd shut it down and take it offline but leave backup power cells online to run life support and other secondary functions they might need. He lit up a cigar and puffed on it a few times. He felt antsy. He couldn't put his finger on why, but he felt the need to hurry up and enter the rift. He knew Morozov felt the same way. Her body language screamed it. She'd been sitting on the edge of her seat, one leg bouncing constantly, hands flitting about as she talked, and she was talking far more than was normal for her. Plus, she kept double checking readouts with Ariana, which she never did. Once was always enough for her. She trusted Ariana.

"Goddamn," Bryan muttered. "She's wound tighter than a choker on a fat chick."

While walking through the hallway, his thoughts wandered to Esther. He hoped Miko had the girl sedated and on her way to the cryo pod, but just in case, he decided to swing into medical and see if Miko needed any help moving Esther if she wasn't done already. As he approached the entrance to medical, he spotted something out of place.

There were bright red splotches on the floor in front of the door and leading down the hallway toward the rear of the ship. Bryan slowed and moved forward, taking short, intentionally heel-to-toe steps, trying to be silent as he approached the entrance. He stared at the red areas, attempting to confirm his suspicions.

Blood, he thought. *It's fucking blood. And those are handprints. Small hands. Those others are small circular splotches and maybe drag marks ... Fuck me! Someone's on their hands and knees and bleeding ... or covered in someone else's blood ...*

He reached the door, pressed the plate, and it slid out of the way. Bryan peeked his head in and immediately noted a pool of fresh blood on the hard ceramic floor, which he followed to its source— Miko's head. He could see that her forehead was split open and swollen, but it appeared the bleeding had stopped.

Stepping around the blood, Bryan approached Miko and knelt down next to her.

"Miko?" he said, touching her shoulder and giving a little shake. "Can you hear me, Miko?"

Her eyelids fluttered open, and she looked over, locking eyes with Bryan.

"Esther," she said. "She drugged me, then beat the fuck out of me with one of my medical hammers."

"Well, I'll be damned," Bryan said. "Didn't think she had that kinda violence in her."

Miko sat up and touched her forehead with one hand.

"Look at me," Bryan said, and Miko squared her body to his. "Man, the swelling is already going down, and it looks like the split is healing."

"Yeah, I'm healing faster than before, even. Although, I must admit, if my bones weren't already denser, she might have done more than crack my skull." Miko stood, grabbed a handful of sheets off the bed, and wiped her face. "We need to find Esther," she said. "I'm betting she's going to the escape pod. And she can't be moving too fast. She's crawling on her hands and knees."

Miko managed to walk to her drug cabinet, retrieved an auto-injector and sedative vial. She inserted the vial and slipped the injector in her pants pocket.

"Okay," Miko said to Bryan, walking toward the door. "Let's go find her."

"Roger that." Bryan stuck the cigar in his mouth, and as he followed after Miko, he called Morozov over the comms systems. "Boss? You there?"

"Yes, Bryan," Morozov answered. "Go ahead."

"Miko and I are trying to track down Esther. She attacked Miko in the medlab and fled. We think she's headed for the escape pod."

"God ..." Morozov said, then paused, holding her breath for a few seconds before releasing a loud sigh. "Okay. It is what it is. We're going to start moving toward the rift now, using thrusters only. I need you to continue on with your assignment, Bryan, and shut the main engine down. If Miko is up to going after Esther, let her do it, but you've only got maybe five minutes before we cross over."

"Copy that, boss," Bryan said. "We're on it. Out."

Miko had slowed to walk next to Bryan while he spoke with Morozov. Bryan turned his head and looked down at her.

"Well," he said, "you heard the lady. When we get to the airlock, I'll continue to the engine room and you can head for the escape pod."

Miko nodded and they picked up their pace. When they were about ten meters from the junction, Esther crawled out of the suit locker next to the airlock door, suit on along with the helmet. She looked right, then left, and froze, staring at Bryan and Miko, her jaw slack and eyes wide at the sight of Miko.

"There she is!" Miko yelled and took off.

Despite her injuries, Esther scrambled to open the airlock, then crawled inside and shut it, her body fueled by fear and adrenaline. Once inside, she stood and locked her crewmates out.

Afterwards, Esther held on to one wall to keep herself upright as she backed up until she was even with the controls. She did not prepare the airlock for a standard opening by depressurizing it. Instead, she opened the yellow plastic square covering the safety override switch and flipped it off, disabling the airlock safety protocols. Esther then grabbed the handle of the emergency airlock release lever and stared at the small window in the door, where Miko's face looked back at her.

"Goddammit!" Bryan shouted. "I've *got* to get to the engine room now! You're gonna have to handle this on your own, Miko. I'm sorry."

"Go," Miko said. "I'm good."

Bryan nodded and took off running.

CARLOS OPERATED THE THRUSTERS, MAKING MICRO-CORRECTIONS TO keep the Evangeline moving in a straight line toward the rift. Ariana monitored the readings coming out of the rift. The signal had not changed in strength or composition, but it was gradually cycling faster and faster, a palpable urgency intensifying with each second.

Morozov felt it too. She was standing now, uncaring of whether she was belted in at the moment they crossed over into the rift.

"God, it's beautiful," Morozov said aloud. "And my body feels electric, more alive than I've ever felt. *Ever.* Do you feel the same, Ariana?"

Ariana's intellectual stoicism faltered, and the pure ecstasy and excited anticipation she felt showed through as she looked at Morozov, a broad smile on her face, and nodded vigorously.

"I feel it too, Captain," Carlos confessed. "It's amazing. I want to gun it and get to the other side now!"

"I know," Morozov said, "but we have to wait for Bryan to shut the primary engine down as a precautionary measure and just leave life support systems running on the backup cell."

"I know," Carlos said. "I just want him to hurry up so we can go."

As if on cue, the main power turned off, and only backup systems remained operational.

"Captain, this is Bryan. Do you copy?"

"Go ahead, Bryan."

"Primary engine turned off and secured. You copy?"

"Good copy, Bryan. You and Miko get up here quick. We're closing on the crossover point fast."

"On my way," Bryan responded.

"Okay, Carlos," Morozov said. "Let's break on through to the other side! Bump up the thruster power by ten percent. It's time to find out just what we will become."

"Roger that, Captain!" Carlos said, excitement pervading his voice as he adjusted the thrusters.

ESTHER AND MIKO STARED AT EACH OTHER FOR WHAT FELT LIKE AN eternity, a slow-motion subliminal standoff. Miko's eyes seemed to war for control over Esther's will, vying for mental dominance. Esther, however, refused to submit to Miko's budding telepathic attempts to break down her determined resolve. Esther didn't bend to Miko's wishes. Instead, she set her jaw like flint, stiffened her spine, and planted her feet like a mountain. Unmoving.

"Captain, this is Bryan. Do you copy?"

The radio traffic appeared on the inside of Esther's helmet, the words scrolling up. Neither Esther nor Miko looked away from one another.

"Go ahead, Bryan," Morozov responded. "I copy."

"Primary engine turned off and secured. You copy?"

"Good copy, Bryan. You and Miko get up here. We're closing on the crossover point fast."

"On my way," Bryan responded.

"You should go," Esther said to Miko, gripping the emergency airlock release handle with one hand and signing what she could with the other. "Seems like we don't have long."

"No," Miko answered and signed through the small window with one hand, the other arm hidden. "Not without you."

Miko's free arm moved toward the door control panel.

"Don't," Esther shouted. "I've disabled the safety protocols. If you open that door, I'll blow us both out the airlock," she signed.

Miko's arm stopped moving toward the panel, and she instead reached out, placing her palm against one side of the window as she took a step and leaned in, bringing her face up to the glass next to her hand.

"Esther," Miko said, making sure to enunciate the words clearly even as her face pleaded for reason and rationality to prevail. "You're not well, Esther. We know that now. Your unique condition has caused the signal to do harm to you instead of great good."

"Great good?" Esther spat out the question and half laughed at the idea. Shaking her head, she released the handle and signed with her thickly gloved hands as best she could, her movements agitated. "Are you nuts?" she yelled, leaning her shoulder into the wall for support while she signed. "Y'all aren't even human anymore! Don't you know that? You should be dead right now, but here you stand."

"Esther, please," Miko begged, "just hear me out, please. I don't want to hurt you. None of us do. We were going to sedate you and place you in the cryo unit in the escape pod so you wouldn't be conscious when the ship enters the rift. We want to protect you. Please, please let me protect you. Perhaps even save you. I can feel it.

It's glorious in there. I believe when we reach the source, it won't matter that you're deaf. I think the source of the signal is going to make us all whole, you included. It's going to perfect us mentally, physically, and emotionally. There won't be any pain or suffering. It's going to be heavenly … But we don't have any time to waste, Esther. We *have to* go. The Evangeline is headed into the rift. It will cross over in the next few minutes or less. We need to—"

"I am *not* going into that rift!" Esther yelled and signed, her movements forceful. "*I will not!*" She gripped the emergency airlock release handle tighter and spoke as if she were swearing an oath. "No matter what. So, you can keep your heaven, you crazy bitch. I don't want it."

Esther pulled the handle down in a sharp, hasty movement. She saw Miko's jaw drop as the airlock opened and sucked Esther outside into space. It was as if the gods of darkness inhaled and she was instantly ripped away.

Miko's face shrunk, blurred, and became a black dot framed by white light within two seconds as Esther's body moved at a high rate of speed away from the Evangeline on a parallel path to the rift. She turned her head to look at the Evangeline as it touched the filmy membrane covering the rift and separating their reality from whatever existed on the other side.

I'm going to die, Esther thought, *but I'll still be me. I won't be something else. Something not me. Something … corrupted.*

She smiled and breathed easy, realizing she couldn't feel the signal assaulting her body. Away from the receiver dish and the ship's metallic structure conducting and amplifying the signal, she felt nothing now. Nothing but relief after days of constant pain. She was adrift upon the void of space and destined to die in a short time, but Esther accepted that fate. She could die halfway content knowing she was not going where her shipmates were headed.

She stared at the Evangeline breaking through the membrane. For a moment, it looked as if the bow of the ship stretched and elongated, but then it was hidden by the rippling colors of what could have been the cell wall of a cosmic amoeba sucking the ship into its body to digest, or a cellular structure sent by the universe's defensive systems to devour those beings which should not be here, who were not worthy to tread these star ways.

Esther suddenly felt aware of her shipmates' coming fate as the Evangeline slipped through the rift. It wasn't a detailed or crystal-clear vision, but she had a general premonition that their end would be a horrible one indeed.

A part of her simply knew in that moment that the Evangeline entering the rift was more akin to spoon feeding a starving colossus, the ship smoothly proceeding into an unknown alien gorge as it stretched toward them, hungry and waiting to feed upon them all. Esther feared for her friends but felt thankful she was no longer among them.

She closed her eyes and breathed in slowly, out slower, conscious of her body travelling through space, farther and farther away from something ancient and ravenous that lay waiting on the other side. She thanked God she was not on the Evangeline as she sailed through the void of space.

And then Esther's eyes snapped open—wide and brimming over with terror.

She was slowing down.

7

BRYAN CAME RUNNING up to the airlock. He saw Miko from a distance, seated on the floor and leaned against the airlock door, face in her hands.

"Miko," Bryan called out as he approached. "Is Esther still in there?"

Miko looked up, tears flowing down her cheeks. All she could do was shake her head.

"Are you saying Esther blew herself out the airlock?" he asked, coming to a stop in front of her.

Miko looked down and nodded her head.

"Jesus tits!" Bryan said and wiped his forehead. "Goddamn. That's more fucked up than fingering your sister and finding your daddy's wedding ring. Geesh." He squatted down on her eye level. "Miko, it's not your fault. Esther made up her own mind. You couldn't have stopped her."

Miko looked at Bryan, her eyes two burning coals. He felt suddenly uncomfortable and warm inside.

"C'mon, Miko. Captain said for us to get to the bridge and pronto." He stood and held out a hand, but Miko slapped his hand away, stood on her own, and took off running toward the bridge.

"Goddamn," Bryan muttered as he hurried behind her. "Signal sure hasn't thickened anyone's skin around here."

Miko entered the bridge with Bryan right behind her. When Miko didn't announce them, Bryan did.

"We're here, boss."

Morozov didn't look at him. Her eyes were glued to the large drop-down display screen mounted to the ceiling above Carlos's pilot seat.

"Good," she said, and nothing else.

Miko stepped forward and grabbed the back of the captain's chair to steady herself, while Bryan sat down at Esther's station and buckled himself in before turning in the chair to look at the screen.

It was so close now. The red and purple interior of the rift was bulging outward, the surface shiny and undulating as if synchronized with another steady pulsation.

A beating heart, perhaps, Miko thought.

The colors moved within the membrane, invading and displacing one another even as more colors erupted onto the surface, creating their own eddies and currents competing with the rest. Over the taut, shiny membrane lay the last remaining criss-crossing strands, the final vestiges of their reality resisting the intruding presence from beyond as it steadily pushed them aside.

"Lord have mercy," Bryan said. "It's … it's beautiful."

"Captain?" Carlos said, doubt entering his voice. "Our intercept rate just increased—without me speeding up."

"Huh?" Morozov grunted, her attention dragged away from the rift. "What do you mean?"

"It means," Carlos began, "the rift is moving toward us now."

"He's right, Captain," Ariana said. "It's not dramatic, but the change is there."

"Captain," Carlos said. "Entering the rift in five ... four ... three ... two ... one ..."

The point of the ship's bow collided with the membrane, and the rift instantly lurched forward, a gaping maw opening up to slide over the hull, to consume it and draw it inside. Seconds later, the ship was gone, the membrane responding as if a small rock were thrown into a pond, the force creating gentle waves which fled away from the center until their strength left them and they sank into the black of space.

*W*HAT THE FUCK? E*STHER THOUGHT. *I'M SLOWING DOWN. *W*HY THE FUCK *am I slowing down? It makes no sense. An object in motion will remain in motion until acted upon by another force. There's no gravitational force out here. None. I should be drifting at a relatively steady rate until I crash into some piece of debris or come within range of the gravitational forces of a planet, moon, star, or black hole. Something with sufficient mass to create its own gravity.*

She swung her head side to side and scanned around, looking for a logical explanation when there wasn't one. At least not one that fit within the box that governed her reality. Esther refused to give up on finding a reasonable explanation, but the rift was the only variable at play.

It can't be the goddamn rift! she thought. *How could something that wasn't producing a gravitational pull suddenly start? How? If something exists within our universe and has sufficient mass, then it will also have a gravitational pull ... but you can't turn it off and on at will. It either has mass or it doesn't. It either produces gravitational forces or it doesn't. But there's nothing else to explain what's happening. It has to be the rift. It has to be. But how? Why?*

And why the fuck am I even asking why? This is the depths of space. A black, primordial abyss with dead matter swirling about an entropic drain hole that ends in the destruction of all that is billions of years from now. "Why" doesn't even compute. There's no intelligence. No reason. No purpose. Matter just is. The rift just is. The signal just is. Us being in the wrong location at the right time is just coincidence. It's all just chance. Cosmic level bad luck.

Esther shut her eyes tight, not wanting to see the rift any longer. Miko appeared at once in her mind's eye, a manifestation of doubt to poke at her feeble conclusions.

If that's true, Miko signed, *then why are you so damn scared of it? Why did you just blow yourself out the goddamn airlock to get away from it? And why are you pissing your pants right now?*

Esther felt the warmth spread across her inner thighs as it soaked into the insulating fabric of her suit.

I'll tell you why, Miko signed, *but you already know the answer to all those questions. They're one in the same, and the answer is the same. You're terrified because you know the "why," Esther. It wants you. It wants us all, and that includes you. It won't be happy without you, Esther. That's why you're slowing down against all laws of physics. That's why it's coming for you right now, when you know the fabric of our reality can do no such thing. The source of the signal* **wants** *you, and by sheer force of will, it's making it happen.*

"Shut up!" Esther yelled in her suit. "You're just a projection ... of my fears ... my irrational thoughts ... Stop it!"

Then why's it getting closer, Esther? Miko asked. *Look ... See.*

Esther opened her eyes to look at the rift and instantly realized she was moving *toward* the rift, or it was moving toward her ... or both.

I'm caught in its web, Esther thought. *I entered its space, its sphere of influence, and now I'm trapped like a ship in the grip of Charybdis, spiraling down toward a hungry abyss.*

Ariana appeared beside Miko and signed to Esther. *There's no escape. Once you enter its domain, it will lead you in the way of death, but the exact moment you perish, you will not know, though you will already be dead. You were dead before it began. You lived though you were dead already and died though you thought you lived.*

"No!" Esther screamed and closed her eyes, but Miko and Ariana were still there before her as if plastered across her retinas, inescapable. "Get out of my head! Get out! *Get out!*"

You know the end of all matter, Esther, Ariana signed. *The bottom of the entropic abyss. The source and the end. The alpha and omega. All things issued from the source, and all things will return eventually. Today, it is you who returns. You and all your little friends too.*

Esther looked at the rift again.

My God, it's gotten so close, so fast.

She stared at the pulsating maw expanding towards her, the membranous opening stretched taut, its multitude of colors aglow with startling beauty, the edges elongating toward Esther like lips parting to bite and capture their prey. The sight of it pierced Esther's heart through and through. Her eyes slammed shut, and the fist-sized muscle beneath her breastbone began beating at a flat-out sprint, like a wounded deer running hither and thither, eyes bulging wide as it tried to outrun the unseen predator, all the while not knowing an arrow had already done the job.

Oh God, oh God, oh God! I can't let it take me! I can't let it take me!

Her legs and arms paddled sporadically as if attempting to both crawl out of the space suit and backpedal through space simultaneously.

Her efforts were futile. She imagined the rift drawing closer, their intercept speed increasing, faster and faster. And then she imagined Bryan floating above her, looking down with a smartass smirk on his face.

Ain't no escape from this one, short stuff, he signed to her. *You're caught up in one doozy of uh goat ropin' now, I tell ya. I mean uh **real** doozy.* Bryan laughed at Esther and shook his head. *Bless your heart. Unh. You hearing this, Cap?* Bryan turned his head, and Morozov was there next to him, looking down at Esther, sympathy in her eyes … and pity.

You still believe there's nothing out here? Morozov challenged her conscious mind. *No wizard behind the curtain? No puppet master pulling strings? No intelligence on the other side of the veil, benign, malig-*

nant, or otherwise indifferent? And what if it is indifferent ... except when it hungers? Can you feel it, Esther? Can you feel it hungering for us? For you? Can you feel it stalking forward as you quiver and bleat like the sheep you are, sweet Esther? Look up, little lamb. Look up and see. The end is nigh.

Esther opened her eyes again. The membrane of the rift was nearly on top of her.

Oh God, it's real, she thought, terror racing through her body like an electric current, causing her flesh to contort and spasm wherever the fear flowed. *It's fucking real. I can't ... I can't let it take me to that other place ... No, no, no! Hell no! I'd rather die!*

"I'd rather die," she yelled out loud, grabbing her helmet and twisting it.

The seal broke. The air blew out into the void. A cold like nothing she had ever experienced slammed into the skin of her face and scalp and rushed down along her upper torso, paralyzing her lungs. She tried to breathe but couldn't. Esther's eyelids froze open, and her eyeballs began to crystallize, and just as she embraced her coming death, she saw the rift lunge forward.

It flowed over her body, all its colors enveloping her at once. In a single moment, she passed through the membrane. And in that moment, Esther knew whatever lay on the other side, it did not desire obedience over sacrifice. In fact, it didn't care about sacrifice. It would take by force what it was denied. Just like it took her.

A dense darkness embraced Esther, squeezing her as if in a cocoon or birth canal of sorts. And then there was a light ahead, far away. She was moving toward the light. Not by an act of her own will but by the contractions of the very darkness around her, pushing her in that direction. She felt a palpable dread at the sight of it, but she could not close her eyes and she could not look away. There was only the black tunnel and the light at the end, growing brighter the nearer it drew to her.

She was not sure if it was seconds or minutes or longer, or outside of time entirely. It simply didn't feel long to her, but she had no way to judge. Her fear mounted exponentially, climbing to dizzying heights, and before she knew it, the light was so bright and so close, there was nothing else.

In that instant, against the will of every fiber of her being, she passed into the light.

And then ... all she knew was pain.

FOR THE FIRST time in her existence, Esther could hear, and what she heard were the screams of her shipmates. *There must be an atmosphere here*, she thought. *For me to hear their screams or anything else.*

She tried to focus on the surroundings and not the screams of her friends. The feral, untamable, teeth gnashing, tongue biting, mouth foaming, screams of rabid, suffering psyches reverberated all around her. Her stomach churned with revulsion and fear while her mind was over-stimulated, driven to the edge of madness; but in the midst of the hell around her, Esther found something else to latch hold of with all the sanity she could muster. Beneath her shipmates' cries, behind those sounds, was the signal, louder than she could have ever imagined, vibrating in her bones.

At first, the signal rewarded her with intense pleasure as it fully washed over her, submerging her in its harmonic vibrations and suspending her in the orchestral depths of multitudinous frequencies. It distracted her from the screams for a time. But then what had bestowed pleasure now brought pain. It invaded her lips and nostrils and began to burn, to consume her from the inside, filling her mouth and sinuses, then rushing into her lungs, smothering her. And just when she thought her chest might swell and burst, it over-flowed and pushed its way down into her stomach and coursed through her bowels.

That was when agony struck Esther like a fast ball pitch to the gut ... and she screamed too, attempting to expel the signal and its pain from her body. Screamed so long and hard her vocal cords should have ruptured, but the signal was already altering her DNA, strengthening her tissues. It constantly healed them, perfecting her flesh and mind, preparing her for unification with the source, just like her friends.

The screams of her shipmates ended one by one. It was then that Esther realized the only screaming she heard now was her own. It was a new experience. She had never heard herself scream, or cry, or moan, or wail ... or beg for relief. Not until now. But after an unknown period of time that felt as if it were a lifetime, Esther realized that the quality and tone of her screams changed.

What had originally been mere experiential expressions of suffering, anguish, grief, and regret was now becoming something different, something more. Her screams were undergoing a meta-morphosis, a transmutation, transfiguring her into a new being, a new creature destined to emerge from this chrysalis of pain once the process of transubstantiation was complete.

Within the signal's cocoon, Esther's screams became the glorious expression of cathartic release, a victorious wailing into the void as the entirety of human suffering experienced during her brief but unforgiving lifetime was forced to release her. Esther knew in that moment what all this pain was and what it was for. This was the death knell of affliction, misery, and grief, the death throes of anguish and adversity, the end of work and the beginning of eternal rest.

As she wailed with relentless fervor, she knew that through the horrendous pain she was experiencing now, the agony of her *entire* human existence was actively being expelled from her body, mind, and soul. What was transpiring would soon be a true and complete transfiguration.

Her final screams rent the cocoon of existential dread that had been gnawing at her bones since her youth, and she broke through. Broke through to the other side, to an existence which spoke of hope and joy, of a new world she could finally call home, where bliss and beauty reigned, where rest and comfort could be found at last.

Colors erupted across her retinas, roiling, billowing clouds of fantastically vivid purples, blues, and pinks mixed with blazing red-orange hues, all brightening and darkening into a shimmering glow eclipsing all that came before ...

Now, there was only beauty to fill her eyes and ears. The sounds and colors of the signal accompanied by the hypnotic, cosmic lullaby sensations of its vibrating bass, soothing her into a state of perfection one could quite rightly call heaven without being accused of falsehood.

She thought briefly of her companions, hoping they were as happy as she and that they felt at home. But the thought was fleeting and soon eclipsed by the monumental glory of the signal emanating from its source, a source of not merely colossal proportions but colossal on a galactic scale.

She witnessed the source with new eyes and ears and was struck at once by a sense of reverential fear, wonder, and beauty. Light years away from her, she saw an orb of planetary proportions. It was a beast of one thousand eyes, one thousand tentacles flailing with coronal symmetry, and one thousand fleshy appendages forming flutes piping in wild abandon and horns sounding in unison to form the signal that had drawn every living entity now trapped within the spiraling web surrounding it. Every living thing that now fed it.

The radius of the web's circumference seemed to stretch to infinity's borders like rings around Saturn expanding outward forevermore, adding ring upon ring, layer upon layer, but measured in light years within this alien dimension called home to the Source and its Signal, to an idiot god and his innumerable piping flutes ... and also to all those intelligent lifeforms who answered the invitation to join it here, who provided sustenance for the Source, now and forevermore. An everlasting feast, which shall never perish or fade away.

In that place, at the current periphery of its circumference, Esther and her shipmates would dwell for life eternal. Together amongst millions of billions of trillions of lifeforms, stretching out in all directions from the Source, they formed an interconnecting network constructed from the catatonic living corpses of the Source's children. Now returned to it at last, they all floated in the void, eternally alive. Preserved by the Signal's transformative renewing power, they all perpetually provided sustenance with the undying power of their souls to the immense, incomprehensible Source of all that is, a being set apart from its creation, unseen but everywhere, ceaseless in expansion and unending in hunger. Constantly calling its flock home to rest and find relief, peace in perpetuum.

Esther's face grew soft, just as those of her shipmates had done when they were swept into the presence of the Source, connected and one with it through the interconnections of all those who came before them. Like neural synapses in a brain, each entity linked to one another until it all led back to the source.

When Esther felt the connection, her mind gasped for a moment, her body too. Eyes wide, the corners of her mouth rose in a smile, her mind calm and at peace, her heart content, her soul eternally at rest and full of joy everlasting.

It feels like home, Esther thought, and then her mind was lost in the Source, a castaway adrift at sea amongst an innumerable multitude of others like herself, each one overcome moment after moment by a sense of destiny fulfilled and a contentment beyond anything they had ever experienced before.

Heaven belonged to Esther and her shipmates now, or what felt like it. Through their ignorance of the eternal sacrifice, they would continually yield ad infinitum from this day forth, they would be blessed with feelings of unending bliss, and they would all live happily ever after. World without End.

Amen.

The End

ABOUT THE AUTHOR

Mike was a cop for almost 12 years, but the last 13 years he's been teaching Military, Law Enforcement and Bodyguards high speed, tactical and off-road driving as well as hand to hand Combatives. He enjoys martial arts and has been a practitioner since 1989 of various styles. Filipino blade arts are his current favorite. Since he was a teenager he's loved reading, writing, and watching movies, particularly in the horror and sci-fi genre. He's also been a prolific reader of theology and studied quite extensively for a layman. He has a beautiful wife who is very supportive and a son and daughter who are both graduated. His babies now are a German Shepherd named Ziva, a Daddy's girl who loves to play... even when he's writing, and a Border Collie mix named Joey "The Bandit" who will steal anything and everything he can, even the toys right out of Ziva's mouth. Mike is a lover of music, as well, and it is an integral part of his writing ritual.

Mike writes an eclectic mix of horror stories and often mixes in elements of thriller and action genres to drive the reader's heartrate up while he explores dark supernatural entities, cosmic terrors, natural monstrosities, and the wicked deeds the human heart inflicts on others as well as our capacity to act against such things. According to Chris Hall, at DLS Reviews, Mike is "a master of utterly uncompromising hardboiled revenge-thrillers." He has a way of provoking a significant response from his readers – whether shock, terror, dread, an uneasy sense of empathy, Heebie Jeebie crawlies or surprise at unexpected twists. Mike will *make* you feel while you read his words. As one reviewer said, when you read a Mike Duke book you don't just read about an experience, you *have* an experience.

Other SPACE HORROR works by Mike Duke:

AMALGAM SERIES
AMALGAM BOOK ONE: CONTACT
AMALGAM BOOK TWO: RETRIEVAL
AMALGAM BOOK THREE: TRANSIT
AMALGAM BOOK FOUR: INCURSION (releasing in early 2023)

Links:

Amazon Author Page
https://www.amazon.com/Mike-Duke/e/B01ICGNKNW?ref=sr_ntt_srch_lnk_1&qid=1558225552&sr=8-1

Patreon Page
https://www.patreon.com/user?u=13849864

Made in the USA
Middletown, DE
07 October 2023